ANDREW REEVES

SKELETONS

PART TWO: THE BALD MAN

Published by
SKELETONS, LLC.

Dedicated to Andrew Mackow

ANDREW REEVES

SKELETONS

PART TWO: THE BALD MAN

1

Ohanzeeeeee, the winged skeleton howled as it crawled from the wreckage of the demolished cathedral, stood with its hooves on opposite sides of the fiery pit and shook off the smoking dirt, bricks and mortar. Hundreds of human-sized skeletons with flames shooting from their skulls and ribs were locked together to make up the behemoth's appendicular and axial systems. It was taller than the naked trees lining the streets and cast a night shadow over the group of Laredoans gathered in front of the massive crowd of horrified locals, policemen and television crews. The behemoth searched the way starving coyotes do but couldnt find its prey. When they gazed into its fiery eyes matching silhouettes of the Golden Gate Bridge stared back at them.

Where's Ohanzee? the skeleton screeched loud enough to shatter windows and eardrums for three blocks in every direction. The crowd ran for their lives. They shoved, tripped and fell over one another. The behemoth turned its horned skull east as its featherless wings expanded up and out to clear the adjacent houses. Once, twice and on the third try they cleared the foundation sending gale force winds in every direction and knocked who was left to the ground, flipped over cars and snapped trees. Without resistance from the night it was airborne, cleared the roofs and soared over the Bay while staying under the weeping cumulonimbus clouds. Splinters of lightning struck its wings to no effect but the rain singed its scorched bones.

Ohanzee, the skeleton howled one last time to wake James from his nightmare of a city he had never visited in his fifteen years living in Illinois. The farmboy was back in another dirty hospital bed and his fever dream was replaced by excruciating pain. Millions of receptors under his skin screamed at his brain to extinguish his second degree burns. He pulled off the itchy sheets to find gauze wrapped around his skinny frame, a needle stuck in his arm, tubes snaked into his nostrils and a heart rate monitor wrapped around his left index finger. What was left of his short brown hair was singed and disheveled and his blue eyes were stinging with broken blood vessels in his scleras. They begged to be closed after probing the room full of dying and dead bodies lying on makeshift cots. Their flailing and bloody limbs reached out but was terrified of their conditions. Dozens of the neglected patients moaned and screamed in the cramped room, down the hallway and on the three other floors of the last working hospital in Stratford County.

Streaks of blood had dried on the walls. Empty IV bags, medical tape, patches of torn clothing and three severed fingers were strewn on the disgusting linoleum. The overhead fluorescents flickered without rhythm and the paned windows facing west were boarded shut from the outside. There was still enough room for one of the skeletons from his recurring nightmares to climb through the gaps between the two-by-fours. Traces of the Illinois morning escaped the broken glass followed by a fall breeze. No birds were chirping but the distant howl of sirens filled the smoky air.

Who the hell's Ohanzee? he asked himself as memories of the winged skeleton flooded his reeling mind. He scratched his head and his ears told him the television mounted on the wall was too loud. He grabbed the remote on his nightstand and lowered the volume of the pretty Chinese woman reporting on a church in the Lower Pacific Heights of San Francisco. She held a microphone with KTVU printed in white, yellow and black. The purple-cloaked priestess had straight black hair, pouty red lips and flawless white skin. The design of her decagram necklace matched the rings on her fingers. Her nails were painted midnight.

Sister Angelica, can you tell us how this ten-pointed symbol, which has taken the place of the crucifix at the First Church of Radiance, formerly Saint Thomas Cathedral, symbolizes your beliefs? the anchorwoman asked while motioning to her sparkling necklace.

Of course, Angelica said and held it up for the cameraman to get a better shot. This is a decagram. Each point represents one of the ten decrees bestowed onto us by Phoebe, the Greek goddess of light, who we worship like Christians worship Jesus. The points are joined by angles, which encase a mirror that reflects the natural beauty of our Sisters.

And what is it about your faith that has been attracting women from all over the globe?

The First Church of Radiance believes the skeletons terrorizing the Midwest are the direct result of men who have kept the world living in sin with their endless wars, corporate greed, technology and pharmaceuticals. Our beliefs, with or without the support of these leaders, focus our unique energies on stopping the age of masculinity, birthing the next wave of civilization in the feminine and building a New Garden of Eden to protect us from the monsters spilling out of Hell.

But what about the accusations that your organization is extorting money from the members' families to finance their room and board in the dormitories on your campus? And to finance your elaborate advertising? the anchorwoman asked but James couldnt take his eyes off the ominous man hiding in the archway of the

Gothic cathedral. His eyebrows were as black as his cloak. The raised hood cast his face in shadow.

I see you.

Who are you? James whispered back and his heart jumped into his throat.

Guess.

He hit the call button to the left of his bed multiple times. When he returned to the news the bald man had lowered his hood and was waving his index finger back and forth.

You... you promised to save my friends and family.

Promises are meant to be broken.

I'll do anything you ask if you tell me how to get them back.

All you need is the book I stole from you and your dead friends back in Laredo.

Where are you?

Dont come looking for me, this is your only warning

Whatcha need? the nurse with Alicia stitched on her blue shirt snapped. She wiped her bloody hands on her twice-worn scrubs and checked his monitors. We got hundreds of people in a lot worse shape than you kid and I'm ready to drop from exhaustion, so I'm only gonna ask one more time, whatcha need?

A pen and a piece of paper please, he said without taking his eyes off the television cutting to a well-produced advertisement for The First Church of Radiance. Hurry, it's important.

Hurry? What's the matter with you? Cant you see all the bodies piling up around here? The mothafuckin hospital's startin to look like a morgue and you're fixin to write a love letter or somethin?

Nurse... please... help me, the old Mexican woman whispered from the cot situated under the window. I need pain killers... anything... my skin's still on fire... please... help me.

We aint got any more, so just sit tight, she said without facing the burn victim. Now, is there anything you really need kid?

Just get me a fuckin piece of paper lady, people's lives are dependin on it, he yelled and slammed the remote control back down on his nightstand. He sat up straight to make direct eye contact with her but she wasnt intimidated.

Dont yell at me kid, or I'll have security throw your white ass on the street. The only reason you got a bed is 'cause you're young.

Without hesitating he grabbed her by the shirt, pulled her in close and stuck his right index finger in her face. Her eyes widened and she tried pushing him away but it didn't work. A pain grew in her belly and she wanted to run to the restroom for fear of shitting her pants.

Listen... Alicia, I'm only gonna ask you one more time to get me a pen and paper or I'll pluck your goddamn eyes out.

When he released her shirt her bowels returned to normal on her way back to the nurse's station. He laid back on the raised bed, put both hands over his face and trembled in fear. Memories of Katie, Saint Michael's, the book of spells, Father O'Mally, his best friends, the Carny House, the tunnels to Hell they opened and Laredo going up in flames came roaring back. Tears followed. His uncontrollable sobbing terrified the other patients but heavy footsteps coming back down the hall kept him from going insane.

Hey kid, here you go, Alicia said. She tossed them into his lap and folded her arms in defiance.

He dabbed his eyes with the palms of his hands and wiped his snotty nose with the back of his right arm. He tried pushing the living nightmare out of his mind long enough to communicate with the irate nurse.

Thank you, he said trying to hold back the pain. I'm sorry I yelled at you Alicia... it's just that... I started this whole mess... the skeletons, the missing people, the fires, everything... it's all my fault.

Oh shit, she said and put her hands up in defense. Shit, shit, shit, are you one of them Laredo boys?

Yeah, we, I mean... I dragged my buddies into it.

Christ in heaven, she whispered and closed the door.

Please, just let me explain.

Shut up kid, just shut the hell up and listen.

Okay, he whispered.

You best get your burnt ass outta here before the newspeople find out. Some pissed off Laredoans have been comin into the ICU lookin for you but Sheriff Dyer or Dyner or whatever his name is has got a couple of deputies guardin your room in shifts.

Sheriff Dwyer?

Yeah, Dwyer's in the room down the hall but it's only a matter of time before somebody lookin for revenge gets in here and sticks a knife in your gut, you hear me?

Loud and clear, he said, grabbed the October 1992 issue of Field and Stream off the nightstand and used it as a writing surface. There was a largemouth bass with a treble hook in its mouth springing from a lake down in Alabama. The fisherman was standing in an expensive boat in the background without a care in the world.

By the way, who's the note for?

My Mom... her name's Jodie.

Yeah, she told me that she was goin out for a few hours to look for your sister.

Beth? Did they find her? he asked while racing down the page in messy longhand.

The hell if I know, I got two family members of my own missin in Peoria. Listen, I dont care what you do just dont tell anybody what I said.

Of course not.

Alrighty then, good luck kid, she whispered and stopped in the doorway. Oh, and one more thing.

Yeah?

Happy Halloween, she whispered and winked at him before shuffling down the hall.

He left the note on the nightstand and pulled the work boots off a sleeping farmer but the sixty-something's chest quit moving up and down when a crow screeched outside. When he expelled his bowels the farmboy stepped away and stole a flannel shirt, jeans and a Rosita High School letterman's jacket from the helpless patients. He cranked opened the splintered window, climbed between the wet boards and fell onto the soggy hospital lawn. He remained undetected by the security guards, local cops and Stratford County deputies smoking under the main entrance awning.

After sneaking across the parking lot he crept down the empty sidewalks and found a small-town living in fear of an enemy the Apostles didnt prophesize in the Bible. There were no children walking home from school in their homemade costumes. No pumpkins sitting on porches. No decorations strewn across the front doors or sticking to the windows.

2

A nineteenth century English Gothic cathedral stood on the southeast corner of Bush and Steiner Streets in San Francisco. Black and purple clouds floated behind the stone decagrams perched atop the peaks. All traces of Jesus, Mary and Joseph, his disciples and saints once glorified in the church's sculptures and stained glass had been replaced with the ten-pointed stars. The new deities and opaque glass promised a different kind of salvation. A hundred and twenty years of storms blowing in from the Pacific Ocean had tarnished the exquisite masonry with streaks of white, grey and black. There was a bell tower on the southwest corner with buttresses on the north and south walls. To the northeast of the facade stood a replaceable letter sign.

THE FIRST CHURCH
OF RADIANCE

A WOMENS
EMPOWERMENT
SANCTUARY

MASSES 9AM & 5PM
MON THRU SAT
9AM SUNDAYS

Not a soul roamed the rainy upper-middle class neighborhood at three o'clock in the afternoon but a flickering light escaped the church's third story windows. Up the marble stairs, past the cathedral doors, down the empty nave, up three flights of granite stairs and past a wood door stood three hooded individuals in a candlelit bedroom chamber. A giant, a beautiful priestess and a bald man gathered around a leather-bound volume stitched together with hair, skin and glue. Its beat up cover was soft and aged. The trio stared into a six foot wide decagram mirror suspended above the stone floor with silver chains running to the vaulted ceiling.

Te rogamus, onipotens lucifer aperire hoc portal ad dominum et ad portandum res nostras ecclesia primum ortus tui, the bald man chanted with his companions. They waved their free hands in the air to draw the Sign of Radiance and the twenty small triangles and one large decagon within the framework changed from reflective to glowing and bathed them in rays of cerise. After a series of flashes the glass revealed the interior of a Roman cathedral where a small congregation of cloaked worshippers held oil-fed torches and staffs. One wore a goat's head. A wretched old woman with a dreadful face and straight gray hair played modal scales on an organ in the corner. Their leader dropped his hood to reveal coarse white hair sprouting from the sides of his wrinkled head. A matching beard half-covered a sparkling ruby encased in a silver decagram hanging from his neck.

Good morning Master, are you ready to come home after all these years? the bald man asked while lowering his velvet hood to reveal himself as part Native American. There were prison tattoos on his strong forearms along with burn and self-harming scars. He closed the volume and handed it to the priestess.

I certainly am Ohanzee, Bauta said with an educated Southern accent. He said goodbye to his servants and stepped through the mirror, lifting the fabric below his silver plaited belt so it wouldnt drag between the two planes of existence. When his bare and dirty right foot was planted he let go of his cloak, placed his hands on each side of the mirror and was helped into the chambers by the nervous giant.

How was your journey? Ohanzee asked, rose and greeted him with a warm embrace.

Most productive, Bauta said, took the volume and combed through it without making eye contact with the others. Angelica, Hong, it's a pleasure to see you again.

Likewise Master Bauta, Angelica said and bowed.

Welcome home Master, Hong said but bending at the waist was difficult for the seven foot tall giant who weighed close to three-hundred pounds. His black hair was straight but unkempt, his eyes were deep brown and his narrow nose was crooked. There was a scar running from his left nostril, through his lips and down his chin. Boils covered his skin.

Ohanzee, I saw that your trip back to Laredo was a disaster, Bauta said. He settled on a section of the book missing pages.

There were a few problems but I reclaimed the first volume and brought you back home didnt I? Ohanzee answered.

You stupid fool, Bauta said, backhanded him and the loud crack filled the room.

Why must you do that Master? Ohanzee asked as blood dripped from his left nostril.

Ohanzee, you almost cost your family their anonymity with your carelessness back in that hick town.

Goddamn you father, Ohanzee said and wiped away the pain with his right sleeve.

Do not call me father.

I'm sorry... Master Bauta, it was a chaotic trip.

I accept your apology... what other news do you have my child?

I spoke with that Laredo kid this morning.

Who, James?

Yes, your crows told me he is heading west despite my warnings.

Well, if he can survive the Campground Killer then maybe he deserves salvation after all, Bauta said. He sat in his high-backed chair and turned his attention back to the volume's musty pages.

3

G'night sweetie, see you in the morning, the man in his mid-thirties whispered and kissed his adolescent daughter on the forehead.

G'night daddy, the girl whispered back. She closed her eyes and snuggled her Teddy bear.

Your son's fast asleep, his wife murmured. She switched off the electric lantern hanging from the nylon straps running across the ceiling of the cramped tent. It died out and left the exhausted family in darkness but there were still other travelers sitting around bonfires throughout the at capacity campground.

Good, he's been fussy all day, the man muttered. He pulled his son's sleeping bag over his left shoulder. Country music was playing on someone's boombox, quiet chatter and the occasional dog barking at things moving in the surrounding forest.

You'd be fussy too if you had a cast on for a month, she whispered and gave her husband a kiss on the cheek.

You feel like fooling around? he asked and reached into her bag. He slipped his hand past her pajamas and into her pubic hair but she closed her legs.

Stop it, the kids will hear us, she whispered and rolled onto her other side.

I know... I just thought it would be fun, he whispered and fondled her left breast but she pushed away his arm.

Go to bed, I'll take care of you when we get to San Francisco, she whispered while zipping up her sleeping bag. Mom says there are dormitories on the First Church of Radiance campus so there'll be plenty of opportunities.

Oh goody, he whispered and nodded off after contemplating his sexless marriage for about thirty minutes. A coyote howled a few miles to the north and its pack responded by yipping but didnt wake them. Hours later the entire campground was asleep when someone tip-toed on the wilting grass outside and knelt by their tent. A slow razor blade cut a vertical slit into the south wall and deerskin gloves separated the opening wide enough so a quarter-inch tube could pass through without friction. Inch by inch it snaked into the warm nylon dwelling until it lay between the children and their parents. The squeaking of a valve followed and a sweet gas filled their lungs.

The snoring father coughed twice but fell unconscious before he could fight off the nitrous oxide. The hose retracted and the razor blade came back and extended the hole a foot. A long arm reached in and switched the lamp back on. Through the opening a rugged but handsome black face with bushy eyebrows, brown eyes, a stout nose and full lips emerged and smiled from ear to ear. His teeth were white and straight. There were patches of gray in his unkempt hair and beard.

Sleep tight 'cause it'll be time for breakfast sizzlin in a cast iron pan before you know it, the man said. Kapran was stitched over the left pocket of his military jacket.

He studied their shallow breathing, eyelids twitching at random and spasming fingers. The little girl kept mumbling the name Phoebe. Drool spilled from her little brother's mouth.

Somebody help me, a woman shrieked outside the violated tent.

The man retracted as an overweight white woman in NASCAR pajamas darted across the campground in hysterics. Her globular breasts, belly fat and heavy thighs bounced in synch with her short strides. Without hesitation she cut through the other sites, stopped by the family's smoldering fire pit and put both of her petite hands on her knees to suck in the October air. Her gasps appeared and disappeared in miniature clouds outlined by the moonlight.

Someone's got my baby, help me sir, she said. Help me, my baby's gone. Please, you gotta help me.

Easy there, he replied and pulled off his gloves one at a time. Catch your breath and tell me what's goin on Miss. There, there, it'll be all right.

Oh thank God you're here, she said and put her hand on her bosom. I woke up and my husband and baby were gone. I tried the payphone but there wasnt a dial tone.

Calm down Miss, just calm down now.

You must be the only one left, I looked everywhere.

No, there's plenty of creatures in the woods.

You mean like squirrels and deer?

Sure, over yonder.

He motioned past the Meramec State Park sign where a heavily worn trail ended and a forest began. The oaks were two stories tall and dense but it was impossible for the full moon to light the understory. A cold breeze ruffled the dead leaves remaining on the branches and the snapping of twigs and raspy voices in the blackness caught her attention.

Who's out there? she asked and took a slow step away in dread.

Oh, just some friends of mine Miss.

My name's Sandy, can you and your people help me or not?

Of course we can, I'm CK, he said while retracting the hose with one hand and looping it with the other but did so without breaking eye contact. When the chore was complete he put the free end into his mouth, spun the valve and took a little pull. He smiled when the effects reached his brain.

CK, what's in the tank?

Oh, this? It's just something to help campers sleep, he said slurring his words but still managing to hang the hose around the valve. Why don't you come with me and I'll introduce you to everyone.

I dont need to meet your friends, I need to find my baby.

Okay, okay, right his way Sandy, he said, put his right arm around her and pulled her in tight. She began to tremble and her heart raced faster than it had in her twenty-seven years.

Get your hand off me, she said and tried to pull his vice grip from her shoulder.

Not until we're done hikin, he said and walked her past other violated campsites and onto the trail. You see, when I went to boot camp back in the sixties, I met a bald fella by the name of Ohanzee. He wasnt like the usual hippie dippie fuckers that needed a haircut. Nah, he was clean shaven, which was unusual back then for an Injun, or what they might call a Native American nowadays. Usually they got that straight black hair, you know?

Stop, I'm not goin into the woods with you CK, she yelped, planted both feet on the pine needle covered trail but he grabbed her doughy left bicep with his free hand. Please, I just wanna find my husband and our baby.

Ohanzee was part Injun, part Southern Baptist and part psycho, he said as they entered the forest. His eyes were black. He had all kinds of markings and tattoos and scars on him. Weird shit. You notice these things when you go through basic together. Hell, I knew who was circumcised and who wasnt by the end.

Where are you takin me CK? she wailed and tossed her head away from him in defiance but it did her no good.

Down to the river, he said and adjusted his grip on her as the canopy blocked out the moon. Now, Ohanzee and I got shipped off to Vietnam together. We was on the Ho Chi Menh trail, had a lot of fun in De Nang. We was in the shit as you civilians used to say. I could never figure out why he was so hard up to reach the DMZ but when we got there he managed to talk me into doin a little recon mission with him.

You sick motherfucker, let me go, she yelled and tried biting his pectoral but he slapped her. By the third time she was more stunned than hurt by the absurdity of his actions. The muddy and waterlogged trail froze her bare and dirty feet. A thorny bush through her pajamas to cut her goose pimpled flesh. She cried out in pain but he dragged her along without a care.

Don't worry Sandy, it's only a little further, he panted. Goddamn, you're a heavy little sow arent you?

You cocksucker, if you hurt my baby I'll kill you, she said with spit flying out of her mouth. I swear to God I'll fuckin kill you.

Like I was saying before you rudely interrupted me, we left our platoon around three in the mornin and it was pourin rain the whole way to some goddamn rice village out in the middle of no-where. Well, we found the hut he was lookin for without waking anyone up. Just like Ohanzee described, there was this old slant-eyed motherfucker waitin on us. Like he knew exactly when we were gonna show up without an alarm clock or watch or electricity in that shitty home of his. He was just a sittin there on his bamboo mat, smokin a pipe with a beat up old leather bound book in his lap. He said come in Ohanzee like they'd known each other for years... damndest thing I'd ever seen.

Oh dear God, she whispered when the forest ended and a clearing lay under the swollen moon. Yellow light caught dozens of skele-tons working at a feverish pace to bind and gag the stolen campers. They dragged them onto the missing sections of a forty-foot wide pentagram carved into the Earth.

So, Ohanzee and I sat down with that wrinkly old gook, took a few hits off his opium pipe and talked about his book, he said and got her upright so she could view the unholy spectacle. Quit your squirmin Sandy or I'll knock your teeth out.

I just want my baby, she sobbed and the skeletons came into focus when her eyes adjusted to the light. Please, just give me my baby and I'll never tell anyone about tonight.

I couldnt understand a word that gook was sayin but Ohanzee was kind enough to interpret. I was trippin so hard on that opium he could've been speakin Spanish for all I knew. When he heard all he needed to hear he stood, drew his military issue .45 and shot that gook between the eyes. He stuck the book in his backpack and we killed everyone in that village when they came runnin to see what was the matter. Hell, we even got back to our squad before the sun came up and went back out on patrol with no sleep. Ohanzee never let that book out of sight the rest of his tour in Nam.

Is that my baby? she asked, searching the clearing to locate the crying infant. Please tell me that's my baby.

Yeah, that's her, bring her over here Jaws, he motioned and the skeleton with a missing mandible walked over to them holding something wrapped in a Dale Earnhardt blanket. It stopped several feet from them and pulled the soiled cloth to the side to reveal the sleeping infant. She had black curly hair, swollen cheeks and a pacifier in her mouth.

My baby, she pleaded but he didnt let go of her. Please, give her to me.

Now hold on Sandy, I havent finished my story, he said and wrapped his right arm around her neck. You see, Ohanzee took that book to San Francisco and I went back to Mobile when the war ended. Years later I tracked down another book, see?

The skeleton pulled the blanket down and a leather clad volume lay on the infant's chest. It was tattered and centuries old. The moon illuminated its nameless cover and darkness crept into the woman's intestines. When she reached for her baby the skeleton's eyes filled with flames and she clutched her belly. She dropped to her knees as blood dripped from her mouth. Flames shot out of her eyes, ears and mouth before she collapsed on the ground.

4

A middle-aged woman with shoulder length brown hair in a forest green Pontiac minivan parked next to a charred cruiser no one had managed to move since the events on October 27th. She shut off the knocking engine but left her brights shining on the Rosita Hospital. She kept both hands on the wheel and dropped her forehead in-between them and sobbed as the radiator let out a puff of steam. In rapid secession she slapped the dash in anger and let out a string of uncontrolled obscenities. No one witnessed the nervous breakdown except a potbellied lawman with an overgrown moustache surrounded by a new beard rolling himself across the wet blacktop in a squeaking wheelchair.

Jodie, I've got something I need to show you, Dwyer said with his Midwestern twang and tapped the driver's side window. His peaked hat protected his burnt head from the weather but his bomber jacket and uniform couldnt cover up the plethora of bandages wrapped around his shoulder and midsection.

Sheriff? Why are you in uniform? she asked and wiped her eyes. You should be restin inside for God's sake.

I know but one of my deputies found this on James' bed, he said and stuck a sheet of raindrop-stained hospital stationary through the opening before she finished lowering the glass. He coughed up bloody flehm into his handkerchief and winced in unforgivable pain. His face was druggy white with bags under his eyes.

What's this? she asked. Whatever strength she had holding back another round of heartache was depleted and streams came down either side of her cheeks. Her stomach sank when she read the messy handwriting.

DEAR MOM,
(AND MEL IF YOU'RE ALIVE)

I'M GOING WEST TO FIND THE BALD MAN.
PLEASE DON'T COME LOOKING FOR ME.
I CAN'T LIVE WITH MYSELF UNTIL
I BRING EVERYONE BACK.

LOVE YOU (BOTH),
JAMES

P.S. PLEASE FEED BLUE.

Dan's dead... Elle's missin... now James has abandoned me, Jodie said and pulled the note to her chest. My whole family's gone now.

Come on Jodie, we dont know how far away he got but I already contacted Special Agent Munn and he's got agents all over the country lookin for him, he said and put both hands on the window sill. So just stay calm and we'll get them a photo of him so he can send it over the wire.

Bullshit, I'll find him myself, with or without you goddamn cops and FBI Agents and National Guard and whoever the fuck else swore to protect us but failed. None of you did jack shit to stop this back in Laredo, what makes you think you can find a fifteen year old hitchhikin around the U.S.?

Jodie, stop whatever you're thinkin about doin and listen to me.

Fuck off Sheriff.

She threw the car into drive but he reached in and grabbed the steering wheel with both hands. She tried tearing them away but despite his condition he was still too strong.

Stop goddammit, he said and had half of his body in the car trying to put it back in park. I'm not gonna ask you twice Jodie, turn the fuckin car off.

She did as she was told, folded her arms and stared at him but her headlights caught something walking across Major Street. It hid behind a maple tree but peered out with two fleshless hands on the wet bark. Its skull was fractured. Labored breaths caused its incomplete rib cage to rise and fall with unnatural movements.

I want you to grab your stuff and get in my squad car, he barked and let go of the wheel. Munn is expectin us in Missouri. He thinks the Campground Killer and the bald man are somehow connected, so maybe if we put our heads together we can figure out where they're at before James gets himself killed.

Sheriff... there's something behind that tree, she whispered in terror and pointed across the lot.

No more games Jodie, do as you're told and we can get on the road. Come on, you can ride with me.

Just look for Christ's sake, she said and slammed her door into his wheelchair trying to get out of the vehicle. Look, look, look.

What did you do that for? he asked as the creature walked into the high beams. Its skull had a hole in it larger than its eye sockets and was missing carpals from both hands.

Where's James? the skeleton asked, stepping over a concrete stop.

Fuck, push me to my car, he yelped and she grabbed the handles on the back of the outdated wheelchair. As they raced across the parking lot she peered over her shoulder. Two more had joined the first. One was big boned and lumbered along with a piece of iron holding its left tibia and fibula together. It held the right hand of an adolescent skeleton missing its left arm.

We want his soul, the child demanded with a shriek.

I thought we killed those goddamn things back in that chapel? she yelled while he fumbled for his keys. The lawmen under the awning drew their weapons and fired on the creatures.

Who said they're the same ones? he asked and climbed inside.

She folded the wheelchair in half, threw it in the backseat and sprinted over to the passenger side. The child let go of its parent and came within a car length as the sheriff hit the lock button. They sped onto Highway Twenty Four in the beat up Ford without switching on the siren or lights. In the rearview mirror the creatures quit their chase to focus on the cops.

When she set her eyes to the west the moon reflected off puddles collecting on the two-lane blacktop but there were no farmers, truckers or locals traveling in either direction. She tried the radio and an advertisement for the First Church of Radiance played through the crackling speakers.

5

Hey farmboy, wanna ride? the blond girl yelled from the passenger seat of a tan Chevy S-10 pulling to the curb on Main Street in Rolla, Missouri. The bed of the pickup was full of bagged groceries, camping gear and three plastic gun cases with buckles on the opposite sides of the hinges. Rust had worked its way past the four-cylinder truck's wheel wells and there was damage to the back right quarter panel. The front license plate read THE HOOSIER STATE. A husky salt and pepper-haired farmer wearing a grubby Indianapolis Colts ballcap and overalls manned the wheel. He slipped the five speed into neutral without turning off the brights as James gave the blond a troubled stare.

You talkin to me? James asked and stepped back so the dirty mud puddle they drove through didnt soak him.

Your sign, the blond answered and caught him staring at her supple breasts squished under her dirty red flannel and Carhartt jacket. Hey, eyes up here farmboy.

Oh, sorry, James said and double-checked his cardboard sign with SAN FRAN written in black marker. How'd you know I grew up in the country?

Cause you look like you just fell off a tractor. I'm Lauren and this is my father Bob, whats your name?

I'm James, nice to meet you both. He took another peek, hoping she wouldnt notice.

I said eyes up here farmboy, Lauren said and slapped his arm.

That hurt, James said and rubbed his left triceps.

I'll break your nose if I catch you doing that again, Bob said while shaking his right index finger at him.

My older brothers taught me how to fight so you'd better be good 'cause we got a long trip ahead of us, Lauren said. She opened the passenger door. Candy wrappers, scrunched soda cans and fast food bags fell out but the passengers couldnt have cared less.

Lauren's all I got left, so if there's any funny business I'll leave you on the side of the road, understand? Bob interjected, raising his bushy eyebrows.

Understood, he said, tossed the cardboard sign onto the sidewalk and got into the cramped little pickup. There were two flashlights, a spiral bound Rand McNally road map, three red Bic lighters, a stocking hat, two pairs of gloves, packages of fun-sized Snickers, Baby Ruth's and Butterfingers, an empty bag of Doritos and a full box of Winchester .38 ammo keeping the two dash vents from defogging the window. The wipers were on a setting fast enough to keep the drizzle from blocking their view.

Where you comin from? Bob asked as they picked up speed.

A little farm town called Laredo. It's about two hours south of Chicago or forty-five minutes east of Peoria.

Never heard of it, Bob said.

But your jacket says Rosita? Lauren asked.

It's a long story, James said with a red face. Where y'all from?

Remington Indiana, Bob answered with pride.

Like the guns?

Yeah, like the guns, Bob said and chuckled.

Are you hitchhiking all by yourself? Lauren asked and pulled a small leather journal out of her Colts jacket. After flipping through the pages she found the section separated by a wrinkled newspaper clipping and handed it to him.

I'd rather not say, James said and studied it. Is this the church out in San Francisco?

Yeah, why? Lauren asked.

I saw this woman on the mornin news, James said and showed them her photograph.

Apparently she's learning how to resurrect people from the dead.

Why would you need to learn that, aren't you a Christian?

Catholic, actually. My mom and two brothers were killed in a drunk driving accident.

I'm sorry.

You should be, Lauren said and laughed at his embarrassment.

The First Church of Radiance is nondenominational but men cant join, Bob interrupted and smiled.

Why not?

Well, we can but it's only in service roles, Bob said and signaled to go around a station wagon full of migrant workers.

That's insane.

You still havent told us why you're going to San Fran, Lauren said.

I'm lookin for somebody.

Who?

A bald guy.

I'm sure you'll find a million of them seeing as how Silicon Valley is just south of the Bay.

Very funny.

So who's this bald guy?

You dont wanna know.

Surprise me.

I mean, we just met and I dont wanna scare you two off... and as you can tell, I really, really need a ride.

Come on, out with it farmboy, Bob said without hesitation.

All right, all right... did you two hear about all of those fires in the middle of Illinois?

The ones that burned down that whole county? Lauren asked.

Stratford County.

What about it? Bob asked.

Thats where I'm from, a rural town called Laredo.

A farmboy from a farm town, how cute, Lauren said and rolled her hazel eyes.

Oh, fuck off.

Watch your language son, Bob said, glaring at him with one hand on the wheel and his right arm across the back of the bench seat.

Isnt that the place where people saw skeletons? Lauren asked.

Yeah, that's the place, James said and rested his head against the foggy window. There were boarded up shops, overturned cars and merchandise littering the sidewalks along Main Street. Someone had graffitied the same word in black paint on the plywood covering the broken windows.

RADIANCE

Are the skeletons everywhere? James asked and the father and daughter faced one another and back to him.

I dont know but my buddy in the FBI said that somebody from your hometown caught one on video and sent copies to news stations all over the Midwest, Bob said in a low register, pushed down his turn signal and double-checked his rearview mirror. One by one the government shut down the stations and they havent been on air since. They're doing the same thing with the newspapers.

So no one else has any evidence?

Not unless there's other tapes or photos that leaked, Bob said.

Are y'all campin on the way to San Francisco? James asked trying to change the subject.

Yeah, why? Lauren asked.

Aren't you worried about the Campground Killer?

Nah, we heard they're close to catching him, Bob said. Besides, there's so many cops and religious nuts and desperate rednecks headed in the same direction that we got nothing to worry about.

Come on farmboy, I wanna hear more about them, Lauren said and elbowed him in the ribs. He tried pushing her arm away but coughed instead.

Stop, James said, flinching in pain.

Oh shit, whats wrong? Lauren asked but did it again. You get hurt cow tipping?

All right, quit, James said and pulled up his shirt to reveal bandages wrapped around his torso. Blood had seeped through leaving dark red stains.

Good God, what happened to you? Lauren asked and retracted her elbow in disgust.

My buddies... I mean, my buddies and I were involved with

the people who started those fires... we ran into those... those skeletons everyone's been talkin about. They killed my friends... my dad and our priest... and burned down most of my hometown.

Holy shit.

Lauren, your language, Bob said and smacked the steering wheel in disgust.

Sorry Bobbio, go on farmboy.

I'm lookin for that bald man I was describin because he knows how to get the people I lost back.

What makes you think he's gonna help you?

I have something he needs. He leaned into the window again and studied a light post on Interstate 44 trying to beat the dusk. There was a raggedy crow sitting at the top. It cawed six times, fluttered its tattered wings and coasted to the dead possum laying in the northbound lane.

And what's that?

I'd rather not say.

The crow pecked at the cadaver, breaking through its raggedy fur. It spun its greasy head and screeched.

Bobbio, should we kick the farmboy to the curb now or later?

Up to you honey but you might wanna keep him around 'cause you've heard all my stories before, Bob said.

6

The First Church of Radiance's pews were crowded with a few hundred mauve-cloaked women chanting Latin on the first morning of November. The orphans, abused housewives, drug addicts, trust fund girls, former prostitutes and aging hippies wore mauve cloaks tied at their waists with silver plaited rope with tassels at the ends. An old wretch played a haunting melody on a Hammond organ situated in the balcony as the modal scales echoed throughout the cathedral. Her protruding spinal column accentuated her hunched back as her fingers danced up and down the keyboard while her body responded with jarring movements. Only a few of her rotten teeth remained. Her eyes were as dark as night and her long and wiry hair was a range of gray, black and white. When the dark hymn was complete she cackled but no one acknowledged her insane behavior.

Thank you Claudia, and thank you for singing with me on this first day of November my beloved Sisters, Angelica said from behind the pulpit. She began to clap and her congregation followed suit.

Thank you Sister Angelica, the congregation said in unison as the priestess lowered the hood of her dark purple cloak.

You may be seated now, she continued and closed the hymnal.

After years of hard work, sacrifice and vetting so many unworthy candidates, the time has come for us to close our doors. Over the next few weeks we will direct new members to our churches opening in Los Angeles, Chicago and New York. Today, I am proud to say that our Master is finally here. And he brought the Fire with him from another time and place. So please, clap your hands and welcome Master Bauta.

The congregation obeyed but turned to whisper in each other's ears. A cloaked old man carrying a leather bound volume in his left hand and a wooden staff in his right walked from stage right and joined the priestess behind the pulpit.

Thank you Sister Angelica, Bauta said and kissed her on the cheek.

My pleasure Master, she murmured and sat beside the bald man in one of the three high-backed chairs lined in front of the high altar. There was a mural of Phoebe in the New Garden of Eden painted on the altarpiece. Her eyes were encased in silver and her pupils were made from glass. Only the most inquisitive Sisters had picked up on the peep holes over the years but kept the discovery to themselves for fear of being punished by the priestess.

It's so good to be in what used to be Saint Thomas Cathedral again, Bauta said with excitement. Back in the sixties, my congregation and I gathered in a little place down the street. We used to dream of owning this church except a housefire drove us apart. Sister Angelica, you have made this once archaic symbol of oppression into a beacon of hope for the women of this country, and I thank you from the bottom of my heart. Now, I know how much you and your families have sacrificed to be here today, so I'll get right to the point. My dear boy Ohanzee recently traveled across the country to hunt down a book written by men much wiser than me, a book that was hidden for decades... hidden from the churches, synagogues and mosques... from politicians and greedy men who have kept the power of the female spirit in chains. Today, I will unshackle your souls with the knowledge contained in this book... today, I will give you the Fire.

As the Sisters whispered in anticipation the Master opened the book, extended his right arm and opened his hand. They fell quiet when Angelica held up her right index finger to her ruby red lips.

Ad ignem Luciferum quaeso manum, Bauta chanted with his eyes closed, causing his right hand twitch and arm shake. Omnipotentis congregationem suis ostendit futurum.

When the last word left his lips a series of sparks ignited in his hand, catching the congregation off guard. They covered their open mouths and recoiled in fear. They froze when the sparks became flames. It multiplied until it was a foot tall but did not affect his palm and fingers. Inside the flame was a black silhouette of Sister Angelica standing in the New Garden of Eden surrounded by her congregation. No men were in the apparition.

Do you see my Sisters? Bauta asked without pain. Do you see your future in the Fire?

Yes, I see it, one woman cried out, clasped her hands and bowed her head. And I'll do anything to make it come true.

So will I, another said and another and another until the entire congregation took in the prophecy.

Then bow before the Fire, Angelica said from the edge of the landing. Bow before the Fire that will put an end to our suffering, grant future generations untold wealth, power and control over the men who have wronged us and bring us eternal salvation. Bow I tell you, bow to the Fire.

1

Jodie... Jodie... you there?

Who are you?

It's Dan.

Dan? Why is your voice so strange?

My flesh... was burned off... I can barely talk.

Oh God no.

All that's left... are bones.

Dan, I'm so sorry, where are you?

Terrible place... with O'Mally... and James' friends.

Where?

Not sayin.

Please tell me.

The Medicine Man... has us... in chains.

Who?

He's evil... wicked... bringin death... to San Francisco.

Wake up Jodie, Dwyer said. He shook the exhausted brunette slumped in the passenger seat but received no response. He checked the rearview mirror. On the road behind them the local sheriff's charred remains were still propped up in his smoldering squad car as the fire department extinguished it with hoses from three engines parked along Highway 185.

I dont know what to do.

Stop him... whatever it takes... stop him.

Wake up Jodie, we're here, Dwyer said.

Where are we? she asked, rubbing the sleep from her eyes.

Meramec State Park, just outside of Sullivan, Dwyer said and took a left onto the winding entrance road.

I was in the middle of a nightmare... about Dan, she said in a panic. She grabbed the door handle to pull herself up and rubbed her swollen eyes.

I know, you kept saying medicine or medicine man or something like that.

He parked between two unmarked Ford Caprice Classics with government plates. A muscular brown-skinned man with jet black hair, a red tie and a dark blue FBI jacket approached and motioned for them to hurry past the television crews. There were orange and white roadblocks across the road cutting through the campground and a group of local police, a crime scene photographer and three forensic specialists scurrying around the violated sites. Local cops pushed the reporters and their cameramen away from the out-of-towners as they took in the carnage.

Sheriff Dwyer, I'm Agent Martinez, he said and extended his hand.

Nice to meet you, he said. This is my secretary, Jodie.

I'll bet you are, Martinez said and chuckled while motioning toward the bank of trees on the north end of the campground. Right this way, Munn is expecting you Sheriff.

Thanks, I just wish it were under better circumstances, Dwyer said and put on his aviator sunglasses while trying to hide his pain.

Yeah, you look like you should be in a wheelchair, Martinez said and chuckled louder than the first time.

It's back in my cruiser so that's what these are for, Dwyer said and popped a pain pill in his mouth. They ducked under the yellow POLICE LINE DO NOT CROSS tape wrapped around campsite number 16. A swarm of forensics were taking samples.

I'd like y'all to meet my partner Agent Rivera, Martinez said when they arrived at the short Mexican man with a thick moustache. Rivera nodded and continued interviewing the campground owner who was sobbing and scratching his red beard.

The wet trail was drying under the afternoon sun but clouds in the west promised a storm. In the surrounding oak trees a flock of crows sat perched on the branches. They cawed and twisted their necks in excitement for their new visitors. Some had bloodstained feathers from wreaking havoc back in Illinois while others were still clean having just merged with the flock when they soared over the Saint Louis suburbs.

Holy shit, Jodie said when they reached the clearing.

Well I'll be goddamned, the Sheriff grunted as Martinez stopped before the singed grass.

A circular stretch of earth forty feet wide was filled with cooling magma. Smoke rolled off the rocks and made its way to the purple clouds hanging above the sacrificial place. A rank odor invaded their nostrils and the agent offered them disposable face masks.

Agent Munn, your guests are here, Martinez yelled across the crime scene to catch his supervisor's attention. Nice to meet you two but I gotta get back to work.

Thanks for your hospitality Special Agent Munn, Dwyer said and removed his sunglasses. You sure you wanna be out here Jodie?

If it helps to get my son back then I'm all in Sheriff, Jodie whispered while pulling the elastic straps around her ears. But, if we're being honest, I want to carry a gun from now on Sheriff.

Not a chance but nice try, Dwyer said, smiled and walked to the edge of the circle as agony found his stomach. Invisible poison reached his mouth. It permeated his senses and made its way to his brain.

You made record time Sheriff, Munn said and pulled down his mask. Good to see you again.

Likewise, we got here as fast as we could, Dwyer said while trying to ignore the painful urge in his bowels. Jodie slept the whole time while I listened to the news.

Nice to meet you Jodie, Munn said but didnt offer to shake because her eyes were fixed on the crime scene. The pot-bellied agent's hair was balding on top, eyes were tired and brown and face was weathered after twenty plus years with the FBI.

What the hell happened out here? Jodie asked, crossed her arms and stood in awe of the wreckage.

Same thing as Laredo, only larger in scale, Munn said.

Larger? Dwyer asked and stuck his sunglasses in the front right pocket of his khaki shirt.

Yeah, larger, Munn said and put his hands on his hips. Jodie, did you bring me a photograph of James?

Here you go, Jodie said and drew his freshman year class portrait from her billfold. He's bigger now... and has a different haircut... but you get the point.

He snuck out of the hospital just as soon as he was well enough, Dwyer said. Here's the note he left.

Well I'll be damned, Munn asked and held the artifacts in the sun. Did he talk to anybody beforehand? Anybody go with him?

Not that we know of, Jodie said. You got any leads?

I shouldnt be sharing this but I got a call late last night from an agent I met at a conference in Oakland a few years ago, Munn said, opened his jacket and pulled out a manila envelope. His wife left him a few months back and he's been trying to track her down but wasnt having any luck. Well, he was watching a news special the other night and not only did he spot his wife in the background... but this man as well.

Who's this? Dwyer asked, took the fax from him and held it close enough for his breath to affect it.

We think it's the guy that put those holes in you, Munn said.

Baldy? Dwyer said and studied the underexposed image.

Yeah, can you confirm that's him? Munn asked.

Hard to tell, it's a terrible photo, Dwyer said, handing it to Jodie.

It's the best my friend could do on such short notice, Munn said.

Where was it taken? Dwyer asked.

The First Church of Radiance in San Francisco, Munn said.

The place we've been hearin about on the radio? Dwyer asked.

That's the place, Munn said.

What ended up happening to your friend's wife? Jodie asked and handed it to Munn.

She drained their bank accounts, cut off all contact with him and their kids and hasnt been seen or heard from since, Munn said and stuck it back in the envelope. They keep all the members locked up in the church dormitories so he cant get in to see her.

Sounds like a goddamn cult, Dwyer said. But that still doesnt explain why Baldy's there.

Maybe he does the dirty work, like tracking down old books in places like Laredo, Munn said. Either way, I'm glad y'all came to Missouri but I'm gonna need you to steer clear until we piece this puzzle together.

What? Jodie asked. We drove all night to get here.

I know, and I understand your urgency, but didn't you see the Franklin County Sheriff burned alive on your way in? Munn asked.

Of course we did, Dwyer said with frustration.

The FBI's got every agent, sheriff, deputy, mall cop and volunteer monitoring these crazy families headed to this goddamn Church of Radiance, Munn said and stuck his hands in his pockets. So we cant afford any more casualties Sheriff.

Any more casualties? We've got nothin left to lose on our end, Dwyer said.

Yeah, my husband's dead, son and daughter are missin, my hair salon was torched and most of my friends and family left Laredo, Jodie said.

Listen you two, Munn said, let his head fall back and closed his eyes in frustration. We did some serious digging and there are some powerful folks involved with this church.

Like who? Dwyer asked.

Possibly the Mayor of San Francisco, Senators, an Army General and members of the Archdiocese to name a few, Munn said. Who knows, they're all just leads until we nail down the hard evidence.

Holy fuckin shit, it goes that high? Jodie asked.

You bet your ass it does, Munn said.

Then let's get to San Francisco and nab them all, Dwyer said.

No can do Sheriff, one step at a time, Munn said. It's gonna take lots and lots of man hours, time and patience.

And how are you goin to pull that off with these... these skeletons wreaking havoc? Jodie asked and balled her fists in anger.

Jodie, I know you're not gonna want to hear this but we have no evidence of those things existing, Munn said.

What the fuck did you just say? Jodie asked.

What more evidence do you need Agent Munn? Dwyer asked and put his hands up.

I know how it sounds but if we spook Baldy, and he's knee deep in this church, it might ruin our chance of figuring out these skeletons, Munn said.

Case? Who gives a fuck about your case? Jodie asked and slapped him with all her might.

Jodie, you cant be doin that, Dwyer said and grabbed her hands.

Well then fuck you both, Jodie said, pulled away from the sheriff and stormed back down the trail.

Nice job asshole, Dwyer said to the agent and adjusted his jacket.

Oh, go fuck yourself Sheriff, Munn said with a cold stare.

No, Agent, fuck you, Dwyer said and stuck his finger in his chest. If you wanna play keep up with the Campground Killer, that's your business but we're goin to California to find James.

A cool breeze shot in from the west and crows landed on the rocks. One by one they spun their heads, screeched at the lawmen and flapped their wings in a primordial celebration.

Agent Munn, you werent there that night in that chapel outside of Laredo, Dwyer said, trying to hold back his pain. Those... those creatures surrounded us... they were real... that bald motherfucker cast a spell and a tunnel... a fucking tunnel to Hell opened up and swallowed that boy's father and their priest and some crazed woman responsible for it all... except they weren't people anymore... they were skeletons.

I know... I read your report, Munn said. I've read every report I could get my hands on, watched every surveillance tape from New York to San Francisco, monitored every lead and got every agent in the U.S. looking for Baldy and James and his sister and everybody else that's gone missing... and the fax I just showed you is the best lead I've got.

He walked over to the sheriff and put his hand on his shoulder. The crows returned to the sky and headed west as the sun highlighted their sleek contours.

Sheriff, we're gonna lose the whole goddamn country if we dont get to the bottom of this, Munn said. Trust me when I say this, the secret to everything going wrong... the missing people... those skeletons... the Campground Killer... it all leads to the First Church of Radiance.

I hope you're right but there's somethin else, Dwyer said and hung his head in shame.

What?

I've been having a nightmare every night, Dwyer whispered so as to not alert the lawmen working around the massive crime scene. I see skeletons in flames... making their way through the Earth... millions of them spill onto the streets of San Francisco.

I understand Sheriff, I really do but you're gonna get that poor woman killed if you keep west. Trust me, she wont make it, she just wont.

Where are we? James asked as he woke inside the S-10 to find Bob parking between a pickup and a 1960s Volkswagen bus painted red. A light mist kept the other campers in their tents, buses and RVs and the office had a CLOSED sign hanging on the inside of the front door.

Outside of Sayre, Oklahoma, Lauren said and pulled her Colts stocking cap on. Come on, we can take a pee break while Bobbio sets up the tent.

Sounds like a plan, he said and followed her down the sidewalk leading to the restrooms. The October night made them zip up their jackets. Damn, it's gettin cold.

No shit Sherlock, it's gonna be an early winter, she said and offered him a Marlboro light with one dangling from her chapped lips.

You smoke?

Who doesnt?

She shielded the translucent green lighter's flame as he sucked on the filter until the other end glowed red. Their smoky breaths gathered and escaped with the wind.

Does Bob know?

Probably but dont go broadcasting it just in case.

It's gonna be rainy in San Francisco, he said, flicked his cigarette and gazed at the stars cutting through the clouds.

They say it always is, she said and caught him staring at her figure. Now, you gonna tell me more about this bald guy?

I'm not sure how much you wanna know.

That a warning?

You seem like a nice girl but what happened back in Laredo shouldnt be repeated.

You're starting to scare me farmboy, she said and he paused to collect his thoughts.

I gotta take a piss, he said, stepping on the half-smoked cigarette. Thanks for the smoke, I'll see you back at the tent.

Okay, she said and headed toward the women's restroom.

He ducked into the men's to find it in disarray. There was toilet paper scattered on the floor and one of the three sinks was over-flowing with water. Someone wearing cowboy boots occupied the far left stall but the urinals were all open. He unzipped and a steady stream came out while images of his hometown flashed through his exhausted mind.

You headed out west? the man asked after he flushed.

Yeah, you?

Nope, nothin but a bunch of peter puffers out there.

Is that right? he whispered and double-checked the man wasnt going to jump him.

Just clench your butt cheeks together when you walk and those fags wont get you, the man said and belly laughed. See you around the campground kid.

God I hope not, you fuckin redneck, James whispered as someone else entered the restroom.

The women's toilets are disgusting, Lauren said in a panic and chose the stall closest to him. Watch the door while I pee, okay?

Uh, sure, he said, shook his cock and zipped up his stolen Levi's. He walked over to the overflowing sink, turned off the faucet and something caught his eye in the mirror.

Are you watching the door? she asked. Farmboy, you still in here?

Holy fuckin shit, he said while studying three symbols carved into the glass. You gotta see this Lauren.

See what? she asked, wiped and joined him while rinsing off her hands in the next sink. What are those?

This is the same symbol as the woman wore around her neck on that news special I watched back in Laredo, he said while tapping the mirror.

That's a decagram but why is that arrow pointing to a pentagram? she asked, pulled her journal from her coat and cross-referenced the brochure.

I dont know but its freakin me out, he said and they locked eyes.

Me too, she said and noticed how blue his were. Time stood still. Their raging hormones responded and they embraced one another but before they could kiss she scrunched up her face.

Whats wrong? he asked with a few inches separating their lips.

Dont you smell that?

No, why?

It smells like rotten eggs... or sulfur... or something nasty, she said, pushed him aside and stopped in front of the closed door.

I mean, we are in a men's bathroom. He rushed to her side but stopped. Something was moving on the floor. A dirty tube snaked between the bottom of the door and the jam was omitting the sweet gas.

Oh shit, I'm not feeling well, she said on buckling knees.

Me... neither, he said before collapsing with her onto the wet concrete. The hose retracted, a valve squeaked and someone opened the door. When James, Lauren and Bob woke a black man sat across from the firepit in the middle of their campsite. He was holding a stick with some kind of meat stuck on the end.

You must be James, he said and smiled. Ohanzee told me all about you the last time we talked but who are your friends?

What? Who are you? James mumbled and tried to rub his eyes but his hands were tied around the back of a collapsible aluminum chair. His ankles were tied to the legs stuck in the mud. He found Lauren and Bob in the same predicament but gagged with hand-kerchiefs. The three of them were situated around the fire at the three, six and nine o'clock positions and their captor was straight across from him at twelve. He rotated the stick to cook the other side of the meat and juices dropped into the coals. Sparks followed the smoke into the clear sky.

Dont bother screamin farmboy, every one of these white trash motherfuckers campin here is unconscious and we're miles from town, you hear me?

Yeah, James said as the nitrous oxide wore off.

My friends call me CK.

CK?

Yeah, CK.

The Campground Killer?

My cock, Bob screamed through his gag and dropped his head to find his pants around his ankles. There was a severed quarter inch stump left below his pubic hair but his blood-stained scrotum was left intact.

Stop fuckin around Bob or I'll cut your nuts off too, CK said and glared at him. I said stop. Dont talk, just listen... good... Lauren's gonna wake up shortly so you need to be patient, okay?

I'll fucking kill you, Bob yelled through his gag as smolder rolled off the campfire and into his eyes. They teared up and he squinted to stop the stinging as he sobbed from the excruciating pain.

Please dont hurt them anymore, they're good people, James said.

Who said anything about hurtin anyone? CK asked. I'm just takin y'all to Ohanzee.

Who's Ohanzee?

You know, that bald motherfucker that wreaked havoc in your hometown? CK said and rotated the stick again. Ohanzee needs your souls so his wife can bring their twins back.

Why us?

Because you're virgins, CK smiled and checked the doneness of his dinner.

How do you know we're virgins?

My crows told me everything there was to know about you but we weren't expectin your new friends. So, we made an exception because she's a virgin too.

We?

Yeah, me and my friends, CK said and raised the stick to draw a circle in the air. From the shadows a hoard of skeletons cut through the neighboring sites missing their campers. All were blackened, missing bones and walked with exaggerated limps. Some had manipulated wire and steel to supplant their missing femurs, radiuses, ulnas and even feet.

Not again, James whispered in dread and fought his binds with every ounce of his strength. Oh please God, not again.

Let me go, Bob screamed through his gag. Lauren woke to find her world upside down.

That's close enough, CK said to the creatures.

Lauren wailed at the top of her lungs but didnt make enough noise to alarm the residents in nearby Caseyville. James almost got his left leg free but tipped over because his other extremities were still tied to his chair. From the ground he witnessed CK reel in the stick and check the meat's temperature with his right fingers.

After serving in Nam, I never miss the chance to eat, CK said and pulled the medium rare penis off the makeshift skewer. Bon appetit Bob.

As he was chewing the skeletons began to cackle, flames emerged in their eyes and chests to light up the adjacent sites. James found dozens of tents slashed, their owners gone and the campground in a state of disarray.

9

The bald man woke to find his wife gone from their bedroom chamber on the second floor of the bell tower situated on the southwest corner of the First Church of Radiance. When he ripped the covers off his naked body he discovered the mattress soaked with sweat. He rubbed his shiny head, scratched his tattooed but hairless chest and swung his legs over the king-sized mattress. His mind raced to put the pieces of his nightmare back together and a chill ran down his spine. He feared for his missing wife. A wavy silver dagger was lying on their mahogany nightstand. He grabbed it, switched on the lamp and noticed the clock read 3:33a.m. He threw on his black cloak, raised the hood and tied the silver tasseled cincture at his waist.

After locking his door he took the winding staircase lit by medieval wall sconces to the ground level, ran into the sacristy and twisted the decagram handle built into the face of the hidden door to the proper sequence. When it unlocked he crept down the winding stairwell and up the stairs to the catacombs. A hundred years of well-organized bones, musty earth and the promise of mortality flooded his senses. He brandished the dagger and walked down the pillared hall toward the flickering sconce outside the last burial vault. Relieved his nightmare wasnt true he found his wife in a black silk nightgown kneeling in front of the stone table where two adolescent skeletons lay facing the ceiling. Her head was lowered and her hands were clasped together as she prayed in Latin.

Angelica, why are you down here at this time of night? he asked and stuck the dagger between his cloak and the cincture.

I was having a nightmare about Paytah and Yoki... so I came down here... I wanted to be with them while I channeled Phoebe.

She stood, grabbed the bucket at her feet and set it on the table where her silver candelabrum cast light over their children. After dunking the wash rag into the soapy water she began scrubbing Paytah's right humerus under the strips of blackened skin stretching down his arm. His charred brain, heart and stomach still lived inside his skull, chest and pelvis. His shriveled eyes were the size of prunes. There were fragments of his former self lying on the dusty table.

Did your bad dream involve our Master? he asked and placed his hands on her tight shoulders.

Of course it did, they always do, she said and pulled away from him to start on Yoki. Her exposed ribs were getting closer to their natural color with each pass.

I was having the same nightmare my love. He took the rag from her grasp, dunked it into the pail and wrung it out with both hands. Don't worry, Paytah and Yoki will be playing in Golden Gate Park before long, just like they did before the accident.

You've been saying that for years Ohanzee... years... but I cant wait any longer, she whispered while fighting her tears. I want our children back... I'm losing my mind while they lie in this tomb.

CK is bringing the refleshing spell to our Master, so it's only a matter of time before we're reunited as a family.

How do you know CK has the spell?

Because the Master sent his crows to confirm it.

He could be lying.

You dont know that.

I know one thing for sure.

And what's that my love?

I know that if we kill Master Bauta we wont have to endure his abuse any longer, she whispered and he dropped the rag on the floor in disbelief. We wont have to play anymore of his sick games in this sick church with anymore of these sick fucking people.

Angelica, have you lost your mind?

No but you have for trusting him... for being his... errand boy... I cant take it anymore Ohanzee. I cant take watching you obey him like a goddamn dog as the years come and go.

I'm no one's dog Angelica, he said and grabbed her by the arm. I do what I have to do so Paytah and Yoki can live again. Until then I dont wanna hear another fucking word about murdering our Master, do you understand me?

I understand my love, she whispered and returned to washing Paytah and Yoki's bones.

10

James found himself sitting next to an unconscious Lauren at the kitchen table of a 1980s Winnebago while a bloody and beaten Bob was resting his sleeping head against the east-facing window. Two patches of condensation appeared and disappeared with each of his labored breaths. On the wobblily Formica table there were plastic plates, glasses and silverware of different manufacturers piled on top of the folded napkins along with condiments, salt and pepper shakers and a clear pitcher of red Kool-Aid. A brown Crock-Pot with a floral design printed on its sides sat beside the gas stove with the front left burner turned to high. The meat sizzling in the cast iron skillet let off a sweet and tangy odor but the chef was gone. Lauren was the next to wake but slow and groggy to study the handmade sign outside the window.

BOBCAT CREEK
RV PARK
(580) 555-2468

It was a beautiful night for early November in western Oklahoma as the fluorescent lights outside the office and mounted on the side of the telephone poles brightened the gloomy campground. The prisoners couldnt communicate through their gags so they stared out the window. The surrounding RVs still had their interior and string lights on but there was no sign of their owners, children or lapdogs. The cabs, side and back doors of each of the middle class campers swung on their hinges. Various articles of clothing, bikes and folding chairs were strewn across the abandoned sites. Smoke still rose from some of the fire pits.

When a crow started cawing from a leafless maple a middle-aged man with a dirty wife beater tucked into his white boxers belly crawled out from under an Airstream leftover from the late sixties. He made his way past a picnic table where marshmallows, graham crackers and chocolate bars sat but the winged vermin swooped onto his back. He tried shooing it away but it plucked out his right eye. The fat old man let out a howl as it stole the other one. He rolled onto his back and covered his face. CK and a tall sheriff with a felt cowboy hat came strolling along with flashlights and scared away the crow. The lawman drew his revolver from his utility belt, cocked it and blew the man's brains all over the grass. After holstering the pistol he nodded at the cannibal and they parted ways. James and Lauren found no solace in one another's eyes.

Help, Bob said but his gag muffled the word. He raised his head and found his daughter and the farmboy. His flannel shirt was torn at the left shoulder and blood had dried down his arm. There were strips of flesh missing with flies buzzing around and landing on the exposed wounds. He pleaded but the RV's side door opened and closed behind the cannibal. He stuck his deerskin gloves in his military jacket, pulled out a leather bound volume from the front right pocket and set it on the kitchen table. The ragged old book tugged at James and his veins filled with toxins.

Y'all ready for some lunch? CK asked while washing his hands with Palmolive in the tiny stainless steel sink. I'm starvin, how do BBQ sandwiches sound?

You son of a bitch, Bob mumbled from the bloody handkerchief.

His eyes flickered and his chest rose and fell with each gasp.

No, Dad, stop, Lauren said with a high-pitched squeal as CK undid the twisty tie atop the bag of dinner rolls. He put four on a serving plate and separated them with his long fingers. After switching off the slow cooker he grabbed a set of tongs from the drawer beside the sink, distributed equal amounts of BBQ on the bread and replaced each top. He carried the plate to the crowded table and handed out the sandwiches.

I'm gonna pull your gags off but I dont wanna hear no screamin or cryin, you understand? CK asked. He waited for confirmation but received none. Not a peep, you hear me? Anyone interrupts lunch and I'll feed you to my Master's crows.

He reached across the table and yanked down each of their gags. They gasped for air and terror filled their eyes as the madman picked up his roll and took a big bite. Brown sauce leaked onto his beard so he pulled his Thanksgiving-themed napkin out from under his silverware.

Goddamn, that's some tasty-ass BBQ if I do say so myself, he said and laughed. I'd untie your hands but I don't really trust y'all quite yet so you're gonna have to peck at it like my crows... come on now, eat.

Oh, my shoulder, Bob mumbled and tried to shake away the flies.

Is my book callin you farmboy? CK asked him with a mouthful. The good 'ole Fire got you back in Laredo didn't it? This book here tore up my insides for years... but I got used to it.

My shoulde... I cant take it anymore, Bob sobbed. Please call an ambulance... please... for God's sake, help me.

Why are you torturing him? Lauren asked and began to cry.

Oh, he's just being a baby, CK said to her and finished his sandwich with one big bite. Go on and eat before it gets cold.

You fuckin monster, I'll kill you when I get free, James said but couldnt break his ties.

All right, all right, CK said and pulled all three gags back over their mouths. Quit your damn squirmin and I'll tell you. Now, there's only certain cuts I like for my BBQ. The shank, rump and shoulder but since we havent come across any pigs, beef cows or chickens, I had to improvise.

No... no... no... Bob wailed through his handkerchief and tossed his head back and forth.

James and Lauren fell silent and stared at her father's shoulder. When the truth settled in they screamed and reared in their seats to get free but all they did was rattle the table.

Fine, if y'all dont appreciate my fine southern cookin then I guess I'll have to keep it all to my damn myself, CK said and stacked their sandwiches on his plate.

$\|$

Agent Munn and Jodie drove past two torched squad cars sitting near the entrance of the Lion Creek RV Park a little after eight o'clock in the morning as the crime scene photographer was capturing the scorched officers. They went a little further and parked behind Martinez and Rivera as a bank of clouds in the west blocked out the rising sun. Their slamming car doors caught the attention of the local sheriff who tipped his Stetson and set out toward them. His deputies were busy holding several news teams at bay while the Fire and Rescue departments tried to make sense of the enormous crime scene. Hopelessness clung to the windless air and dread was frozen on everyone's faces.

Agent Munn, I'm Sheriff Smith, he said with an Oklahoma accent while extending his meaty hand. He was six foot three and his hat was shaped to perfection.

Thanks for holding down the fort, these are my Agents Martinez and Rivera, Munn said. Whattya know so far?

I know that we need to find this son of a bitch before he makes camping the most unpopular pastime in America.

Boy, you aint a kiddin, Munn said as Sheriff Dwyer and Jodie parked behind his vehicle. Well I'll be damned.

What's the problem Agent Munn?

Uh, nothing I cant take care of, excuse me for a second Sheriff.

You bet.

Martinez, Rivera, get to work while I get rid of Dwyer, Munn whispered as he hurried back to the parking lot with a face incapable of hiding his anger.

Sure thing Boss, Martinez responded and gestured to Rivera.

I thought I told you to hang back Sheriff Dwyer? Munn whispered when he was twenty feet from the unwelcome guests. Are you taking too many painkillers?

We caught it on the scanner, Dwyer said as Jodie slipped under the police tape and toward the nearest RV. Figured it wouldnt hurt in case you found James.

Dwyer, let's get something straight, Munn said and put his hands up in defense. This is an FBI investigation, do you understand?

Of course I understand.

Then what the fuck are you doing here Sheriff?

Agent Munn, we've got a horse in this race and dont plan on goin home anytime soon... with or without your approval.

I'm telling you to get that poor woman, get back in your car and get the fuck back to Illinois before I have you arrested for interfering with a national investigation.

Wait, where'd she'd go? Dwyer asked. He tilted his peaked hat onto the back of his head and surveyed the campground. A blond from KVIJ was interviewing Sheriff Smith as forensics were planting evidence flags around the eyeless camper and the firemen were rolling up their hoses.

If she tampers with any evidence it's your ass Dwyer, Munn said with both hands on his hips.

Gentlemen, over here, Jodie said loud enough to get their attention but quiet enough to remain unnoticed by the other lawmen. They rushed over and met her under the extended awning of a Jayco RV with three crows perched along the cross brace. The campers were gone but their folding chairs, s'more makings and roasting sticks were strewn around their site. In silence she pointed to the side of the RV where a word was written in dried blood.

BORDERLINE

That's my son's handwritin, I could spot it anywhere, Jodie said. She lowered her arm and began to cry.

How in the fuck didnt the local law dogs see that? Dwyer asked.

Who said they didnt? Jodie asked between sobs.

The both of you calm the fuck down before you start making wild-eyed accusations, Munn barked. He pulled the manila envelope from his jacket and held the fax at arm's length to compare the two styles.

That's a match, Dwyer said to get a nod from the agent.

Agent Munn, you keep sayin the Sheriff and I are in over our heads, Jodie said, trying to regain her composure. But from what little I've seen, you're absolutely clueless as to who you can trust in this investigation.

I think you're right Jodie... I think you're right, Munn said.

12

CK woke in the queen-sized bed in the back of his Winnebago to find James, Lauren and Bob missing from his kitchen table where dozens of engorged flies were swarming their dirty cereal bowls and spoons leftover from breakfast. Their ties, handkerchiefs and splotches of crimson were strewn across the old carpet floor but they somehow had managed to close the screen and front doors without interrupting the cannibal's afternoon nap. When he grabbed the first handle he stopped and searched for the second book of spells. In a state of panic he turned the kitchen, bathroom and bedroom upside down because he didnt want to accept they had stolen it during their escape. He darted out of the RV and found the Texas sun falling toward the western horizon and the manager he checked in with sometime after midnight draped over the circular wooden sign outside the office.

BORDERLINE
CAMPGROUND
ROUTE 66

The power and telephone lines running from the one story shack were severed and lying across the playground, the surrounding mobile homes were lifeless and dozens of stinking bodies were scattered at random. One was half in and half out of the driver's side of an old Buick with a steaming radiator. Another was sitting against the women's restroom door with blood seeping out of her mouth and eyes staring at the November sky. A group of five were slouched in lawn chairs by a smoking charcoal grill but someone had twisted their necks into unnatural positions. Their tongues were hanging out of their mouths. All were being pecked at by crows who had no intention of abandoning their free lunch.

As he took in the human wreckage a slight blur from the corner of his eye pulled his attention to the creek winding around the tent sites and heading north. He followed the freshwater at a gallop with his heart pounding and sweat falling down his back and collecting under his stinking arm pits. When he breached the property line he side stepped around a cluster of large rocks and the earth sunk into a canyon where the creek intersected a nameless river. When he crept down the bank he tried to stop but his Redwing Boots lost traction on the clay and he landed on his back. He used his hands and elbows to sit up straight and stared across the water.

Shit, what have you done now? he yelled at the horde of skeletons working at a furious pace to drag the bound and gagged campers to flatter land.

Over here, the skeleton without a mandible said and forged the river with the missing book.

Thank God you found it Jaws, what happened? he asked. He flipped through it to confirm no pages were missing.

Caught three escaping, the skeleton said and led him to dozens of terrified men, women and children with torn clothes and disheveled hair sitting at the feet of four other creatures. The clouds above had become pink and red and purple, the temperature was dropping and a breeze had rolled in from the south.

Anybody get away? he asked, tucked the book into his olive green jacket and pulled up the zipper.

No, the skeleton said as James, Lauren and Bob glared at him.

Anybody watchin the road?

Yes.

Then why the hell did you tear apart the entire fuckin campground durin my nap?

Sick of waiting.

I've told you dozens of times not to do this shit durin the day, it's too risky, do you understand?

Yes.

Good, because I cant reflesh y'all if I'm sittin in jail.

It's been years.

It'll be a lifetime if we get caught, do you understand me Jaws?

Yes... I understand.

Good, it'll be dark soon so get to work on the pentagram and I'll deal with these knuckleheads, he said and the creatures dragged away the other prisoners. Once alone he crouched beside the trio, opened the book and located a spread on the ninety-sixth page. He spoke a passage in Latin to summon Lucifer until Bob foamed from his mouth and his unblinking eyes fixated on the falling sun.

13

The bald man spun the decagram handle left and right enough times to unlock the iron door and walked into the dark bedroom chamber. He waited without saying a word to Master Bauta who stood with his back to him gazing into the decagram mirror mounted on the east wall. The portal displayed four figures wearing silver masks and black cloaks with the hoods raised standing in a Roman cathedral with pendants hanging from their necks. The tall and skinny man wore the Venetian mask of Pulcinella which had a big nose but didnt cover his mouth. A curvaceous woman in her thirties with long brown hair hanging past her breasts wore the circular mask of Moretta. It had round eye holes and a dainty nose but didnt cover her lips. The obese black man taking labored breaths wore the half-mask of Brighella. He held a silk handkerchief to dab the leaking blisters on his hands, neck and face. A dainty Middle Eastern woman in her late teens wore the feline-inspired mask of Gnaga with its pointy ears, elliptical eyeholes and whiskers carved into the aged silver. She had fair skin and pursed red lips.

Good evening Ohanzee, has your wife readied her congregation? Pulcinella asked with an Italian accent but the bald man stumbled to answer.

Well, has she my child? Bauta asked.

She's doing everything in her power Master Pulcinella, Ohanzee said and took his Master's side.

Our patience is running out, so tell your wife to double her efforts, Pulcinella said in anger.

The Sisters will be ready, you have my word, Ohanzee said.

Master Bauta, once you know the spell works, please reflesh your grandchildren immediately so we can transport you to Italy to help us locate the third volume, Pulcinella said.

What do you mean works, Master Pulcinella? Ohanzee asked and glared at his Master. I'm confused, I thought the refleshing spell was proven?

Quiet my child, Bauta whispered, grabbed the bald man's wrist with his right hand and drew a decagram in the air with his left. I'll bid you good night Masters, it has been a pleasure chatting with you.

Good night Master Bauta, we'll see you soon, Pulcinella said as he and his constituents chanted and mimicked the sign. Lucifer Deo placet et obstruere portas San igne corda nostra, Amen.

Their image distorted in the mirror until they vanished without a trace, leaving only the bald man and his Master's reflection. A candelabra on his nightstand and another on his reading table lit the chamber where oil paintings of long-dead Masters crowded the stone walls. One was a hairless boy, another was cursed with plague boils on her face and some were young, beautiful and regal. Most had sinister eyes cutting through the evil men.

Ohanzee, grab that bucket from the corner while I sit, Bauta said and walked to the stained glass window. He grabbed the crystal server, poured himself a glass of wine and took a long drink. His decrepit old frame left plenty of room in the high backed chair painted silver with red velvet cushions. He propped his legs onto the matching stool and let out a sigh of relief.

The bald man retrieved the container and took his Master's bony and wrinkled bare right foot. His toenails were long, jagged and yellowed with dirt caked underneath. The hairs sprouting from the knuckles were coarse and white.

Master, why didnt you tell me the refleshing spell was untested? Ohanzee asked. He dunked the rag into the tepid water and wrung it out before grasping his other foot.

Lack of trust, Bauta said and took a sip.

And why dont you trust me Master?

How can I trust you and your wife after she went behind both of our backs and was testing spells on Paytah and Yoki without my authority? Bauta asked and poured another glass. No wonder you're in this position.

What position?

A desperate position, Bauta said and cupped the bald man's chin with his veiny hand. Desperate to undo your wife's mistakes... desperate to win her over with empty promises... desperate to patch your family back together when we both know she will tear it apart again because of her self-hatred.

You son of a bitch, Ohanzee said. He pulled away and tossed the bucket against the south wall. The dirty water shot in every direction as it bounced off the ceiling and broke on the marble floor. He tried for the door but a pain growing in his belly sent him to the floor.

Calm down my child, Bauta said and placed his wet foot back on the stool. No need to get so upset, the refleshing spell will work, you will get your children back and your reunited family will be free of me when our hunt for eternal salvation is over.

Over? Ohanzee asked with a red face. You said this would be over years ago Master... it's been ages... my poor wife is going mad with grief... and depression... and loneliness.

Ages? Bauta asked, setting the glass on the table. You don't know ages my child, Master Pulcinella knows ages, he's been around since the fall of the Roman empire. I met Brighella after the Civil War. Poor, poor Moretta saw the rise and fall of The Third Reich in Germany and sweet Gnaga has seen countless dictators fail in the Middle East. No, you dont know ages my child, you dont know how long the Masters have suffered to correct God's silly little mistakes.

I'm sorry Master, Ohanzee said from the fetal position. Just please... please stop hurting me and my wife.

No need to beg my child, just comfort your insufferable wife, Bauta said and let go of his soul. But do not, I repeat, do not bother me with your marital troubles again, do you understand?

Yes, I understand Master, Ohanzee said. He hobbled to the door but couldnt didnt unlock the handle.

Much like your marriage, only I know the combination to free you, Bauta said as he crowded around the bald man.

Of course you do Master, I was foolish to doubt your wisdom, Ohanzee said and waited for him to open the door.

Listen to me my child, Bauta said as he spun the handle to the proper sequence. When you finally let go of your resentments, fears and desires, the Fire will be yours. Until then, I am your Master and you and your wife will obey me.

14

Under the waxing crescent moon an armored rescue vehicle crept along Interstate 44 with its lights off and stopped a quarter of a mile before the gravel lane leading to Borderline Campground. The muddy white van parked with two wheels in the ditch and two on the blacktop and the SWAT team exited the rear without slamming the doors. Agent Munn drew his standard-issue Glock and led the twenty-four members dressed in helmets, goggles, black fatigues and elbow and knee pads around a torched Oldham County squad car. They carried Remington 870 Express shotguns, Hecker and Koch MP5's and Colt AR-15's parallel to the ground, with their safeties in the fire position and their barrel-mounted flashlights clicked off. Their eyes darted in all directions in anticipation of an enemy they had only read about in confidential reports as they shuffled down the lane.

When they reached the dead silent campground clouds of flies were swarming the lifeless bodies scattered around the violated sites. The stench was so bad it caused the shortest and fattest SWAT member to vomit into the wilted grass without warning. Munn raised his left index finger to his mouth to silence the fat man as he wiped the bile from his mouth. The pissed agent motioned for the team to split up and search the RVs in two-man groups hoping the fat man didnt blow their cover. The pairs ducked in and out of the abandoned campers, checked the slashed tents and cleared the restrooms but found no one left alive. After they regrouped by the office Munn gave the signal to stop all movement and tilted his head similar to a confused hunting dog. Strange words rolled in from the north in slow waves. The team responded by spreading out into east and west teams.

They tiptoed parallel to the creek, down the river bank and onto the gravel shore to find torchlights illuminating the flatland on the other side. The silhouette of a black man wearing a military jacket and holding a book stood with his back to the intruders. He was chanting in Latin as dozens upon dozens of creatures of every size crowded around the fifty foot wide human pentagram repeating the spell with their hellish voices. Some of the skeletons were goliaths, Neanderthals and adolescent children but most were adults. They had staked the squirming hostages to the ground to form the curves and diagonal angles of the unholy symbol with five torches planted at the apexes. Their muffled cries for help reached the crouched SWAT team as the cops found no solace in one another.

God help us, Munn whispered from one knee. He collected his wits, signaled for his men to spread out and they forded the river without drawing attention to themselves. When they reached the ritual he motioned for them to hold their position.

Drop the book and put your hands above your head, Munn yelled but the cannibal didnt obey the agent. I said drop the goddamn book and put your hands up motherfucker.

Go on, get out of here, I'll catch up with y'all near San Francisco, CK whispered to his skeletons and they backed into the darkness while he stayed still. Go on now, these pigs aint worth the trouble.

He closed the book and stuck both hands in the air. The fat man and another SWAT member swarmed him, stole the volume and cuffed his wrists behind his back. Munn noticed three prisoners lying at the cannibal's feet. The torchlight accentuated the whites of their eyes and pleading faces.

Give me that book, get those people untied and call in Fire and Rescue, I'll take care of these three, Munn yelled at the team, brandished his pocket knife and cut them free. Are you James?

Yes, the farmboy said. The agent pulled his gag down and helped Lauren and Bob with theirs. The father and daughter embraced one another while crying tears of joy to be free.

Save it you two, we gotta get outta here, Munn whispered to them and pulled Bob's arm over his shoulders to escort him to safety. Help me with him James.

The four left the SWAT team behind, crossed the frigid river and followed the creek back to the campground. After readjusting their hold on Bob they stumbled down the gravel lane as two unmarked vehicles with plain clothed drivers came to a stop at the blacktop road. Agents Martinez and Rivera were in the van and Dwyer and Jodie were in the cruiser waiting to escort them across state lines.

15

Agents Munn and Rivera dragged the Campground Killer into the men's restroom at the closed Red Rock Park outside of Gallup, New Mexico, handcuffed him to the ceiling mount of the stall divider and worked him over in shifts. When the cannibal's face was swollen, a few of his ribs were broken and his body hung limp Munn washed his hands in one of the three sinks and used the graffiti-marked air dryer before putting on a pair of blue latex gloves. He never said a word while brandishing his Leatherman tool from the Velcro pouch situated beside his holstered Glock on his right hip. He folded out the knife, cut the crotch away from the cannibal's blue jeans and underwear and returned the blade. After he collapsed the handles to expose the pliers he cupped the cannibal's hairy scrotum with his left hand and placed the jaws around his right testicle.

I knew you vets were tough cookies but goddamn CK, I'm too old and too outta shape to keep swinging, Munn whispered in his ear. So no more bullshit, I wanna know why you've been kidnapping campers all over the U.S. for the last few decades, your involvement with those sick motherfuckers out in San Francisco and, most of all, what in the hell were those creatures we saw back at Borderline Campground, okay?

Fuck you Munny Bunny, CK said and head butted him.

Before blood could leave the gash above his brow the pliers bit the cannibal's sack and he let out an inhuman wail. He tossed his head back and forth and bucked his body up and down and left and right trying to get free of the handcuffs cutting into his wrists and zip ties around his ankles. His determination only increased the pain so he faced his captor. Dark red was streaming down the agent's face as he blinked trying to keep it out of his eye.

No, fuck you, Munn said and squeezed the pliers.

Alright, stop, stop, stop, CK begged as his chest rose and fell with each violent breath. I cant take anymore... I'm beggin you.

Go on then, tell us everything, Munn said and reduced the tension.

Send the farmboy in.

Who?

James... you know... the kid from Laredo.

Dont fuck with me CK, Munn said and doubled the pressure.

Send the fuckin boy in... or I'm not talkin Munny Bunny.

Why James? Tell me now you fucking piece of fucking shit.

Because... he understands.

Understands what?

The Fire.

You're fucking with me again CK, Munn said and placed both hands on the multitool. Out with it, what's the Fire?

It's the reason for what's goin on... the books... the skeletons... the church out in San Fran.

If I send that poor kid in here and you so much as look at him wrong I'll cut your balls off, do you understand me CK?

Loud and clear.

Rivera, you heard the man, get James but tell Martinez to keep everyone else outside, Munn said. He let go of the damaged scrotum, stood by the sink and caught the tortured cannibal's gaze in the mirror as he let cold water run over the Leatherman. He tapped it on the porcelain, held it under the air dryer and was sticking it back in the pouch when there were three hard knocks on the metal bathroom door.

We're coming in, Rivera announced.

Dwyer, Jodie and James stood in the doorframe shocked at what had happened to the Campground Killer while they were in the parking lot helping Lauren and Martinez suture Bob.

Oh my God, what have you done to him? Jodie asked and held her son back with two hands to protect him from the harsh realities of their violent new world.

God fucking dammit Rivera, I told you only James, Munn said as the sheriff pushed him aside to check the prisoner's vitals.

He needs a hospital, Dwyer said glaring at the exhausted agent.

Fuck him and anyone else involved with his murdering ass, Munn said and rolled his sleeves back down. This man is a cannibal... a fucking cannibal who's responsible for hundreds of kidnappings and murders while somehow eluding the FBI for decades.

Fuck him? Dwyer asked and put his hands in the air. We're still lawmen, Agent Munn. We still have an oath to uphold.

The rules have changes Sheriff, Munn said and grabbed his FBI jacket hanging on the door hinge. Beating on this sick motherfucker might just get us closer to stopping that shitstorm gathering in San Francisco.

Fine... but no more torture, Dwyer yelled.

Whatever you say, Munn said and leaned against the sink. Now what have you got to say to him CK?

Come closer farmboy, CK said. Bloody saliva was dripping from his mouth as James inched toward him.

Careful, you cant trust him James, Jodie said without letting go of her son.

I saw you starin at my book when we were in my RV back in Oklahoma, CK said. I saw you twistin and turnin when it was sittin on my kitchen table.

Yeah, it started when that skeleton... when Katie possessed me and my friends back in Laredo, James said while trying to ignore his restless bowels.

Yeah, she's a powerful one... she's just full of the Fire but they aint all like that... some are as useless as tits on a boar.

The Fire? James asked and pushed away his mother.

Be careful, Jodie said.

He's fine ma'am, CK aint going anywhere, Munn said and put a
stick of gum in his mouth.

Your soul is the Fire... and the Fire is your soul, CK said and spit
onto the dirty concrete floor. Religion, science, philosophy, math,
technology... all that shit is just tryin to figure out what the proph-
ets, madmen and witches who wrote the spells in my book knew all
along... but they kept the truth about the Fire hidden... locked up
and in the shadows since day one... because the spells are the link
between this life and the next.

Why keep them hidden? James asked.

Think about it... how would politicians, insurance companies,
priests, doctors and lawyers turn a profit if we could live forever?
If there werent any diseases? If we could bring people back from
the dead? It's all just a big con... the Fire is the truth... the reason
for our existence... the reason we live and die and where we go, or
dont go, after.

I just wanna know how to get my friends back.

I'm trying to tell you but you aint listenin, are you farmboy? CK
asked. He raised his head but his eyes were so swollen he had trouble identifying who was who.

I'm listenin, go on.

A skeleton is someone who was sacrificed on Earth... and sent to
Hell where their flesh was burned off... but they cant escape unless
someone takes their place.

So how do you kill them?

You dont.

Whattya mean you dont? Dwyer asked with his arms folded.

I mean we dont know how... well, we know you can send them back to Hell... bury them and chain them up... but to permanently get rid of them... well, that spell's in the third volume... and it's hidden somewhere in Italy.

There's three? James asked.

Yeah, the first brings skeletons back from Hell... the second refleshes them... and the third makes them immortal.

Like eternal salvation? Jodie asked.

Yeah but not in heaven, here on Earth... that's why the third book is so damn important... supposedly it's locked up in the Vatican.

Is that why you're bringin skeletons out of Hell? To build an army? Dwyer asked.

Yeah... the Masters are going to invade Rome when all of the pieces are in place.

How many are there? Munn asked.

Five, as far as I know... they've been plannin this for a hundred and some odd years.

You're insane and so is your bald friend, Dwyer said.

Ohanzee? Shit, he's just a half-breed with daddy issues and a bitch for a wife.

You're all evil incarnate as far as I'm concerned, Jodie yelled, pointing her finger at him.

See, there you go again with that good and evil nonsense... there's no good and evil, there's only the Fire... you gonna waste it on prayer Jodie? Kneelin before some God... or some savior that no one's heard from for almost two-thousand years? Or you gonna harness the Fire and beat death?

All right everybody, the show's over, Munn said and motioned for everyone to vacate the restroom. CK is obviously leading us on a wild goose chase so let's get back on the road.

I might be Munny Bunny... but you asked and I told you what I know about the Fire.

I'll do whatever it takes to bring my friends back, James said and held his hands out to offer himself to the cannibal.

You sure about that farmboy? You sure you wanna give up your soul to bring back a man who isnt even your father? For a priest that hid at Saint Michael's instead of coming forward and raisin you? For friends who called you insane behind your back? For people that were sendin hitmen into the Rosita Hospital for what you done to your shitty little town?

I'd sell my soul to get Laredo back to normal.

Your soul's already gone farmboy... but if you work with me I can help you get it back.

Do you promise?

I promise, CK said and glared at the agent. Looks like we got a deal Munny Bunny.

Deal? Munn asked with a disgusted expression on his face.

Yeah... I help this kid learn the Fire... then you set me free when the time comes... deal?

Why should we believe you? Munn asked. Hell, the bald man promised to bring his friends and family back but disappeared before holding up his end of the bargain.

First of all... I aint the bald man... and second of all... I want to keep my testicles.

You sure about this James? Dwyer asked.

I said whatever it takes, James said.

Good... because it's gonna take that, CK said and let out a sigh of relief. Now somebody cover up my cock before it catches a cold.

16

Lucifer... magna conscia aperi oculos ut videamus medicina... in inferno, Bauta chanted with Ohanzee and Angelica standing on either side of him. They faced the glowing twelve foot wide mirror suspended above the altar in the cathedral. All three raised their hands to deflect the bright light as it transitioned from yellow to blood orange to a weak crimson. After they lowered their arms the portal revealed a makeshift city carved into the base of black mountains where hundreds of skeletons were exiting their rock-cut homes. They took the tunnels to the courtyard where a mirror large enough to walk through was planted atop a pile of giant black crystals. The parents and their children wore jewelry craft-ed from the bones of extinct beasts, jewels stolen from the graves under the living world and metals found in the tunnels leading to the First Circle of Hell. The warriors held spears with arrowheads made from dinosaur bones fastened to the shafts using steel wire.

When the city was empty their Medicine Man parted the crowd and came within several feet of the portal and stopped while he twirled his tomahawk. The iron blade was razor sharp, the handle was a deer antler and the strap tied to the butt was made from the mane of a long extinct beast.

Good evening my old friend, Bauta said. He bowed as Claudia

finished the haunting melody on the pipe organ in the balcony.

Hello Master Bauta, the Medicine Man named Didanawisgi said with a distorted voice and tilted his head.

The Black Mountain Army has grown, I'm impressed, Bauta said, handed the book to Ohanzee and lowered his hood.

More are coming... many more, Didanawisgi said, continuing to twirl his archaic weapon. Where's CK?

Abducted by the law again but the second book will be here soon, you have my word.

No book, no army, Didanawisgi said while pointing his tomahawk at him. I want my flesh back.

Trust me old friend, you'll be walking among the living in no time.

Good... I have a surprise, Didanawisgi said and two of his servants dragged nine chained skeletons from the entrance. The first had the pelvis of a female, two were males and seven were teenage boys. They all writhed against their neck restraints as the servants made them bow to the Master.

I'm aware of the Laredoans who ended up in your care... but is that Katie? Ohanzee asked.

Yes, she said and hung her head in shame.

Why haven't you desouled her? Bauta asked with a booming voice.

She's mine, Didanawisgi said and reeled in her chain to bring her to his side.

You cant trust her, Angelica said in anger. Please, desoul her, I beg of you. If not for Master Bauta, for his grandchildren.

No, Didanawisgi said and brought his tomahawk to Katie's neck as she fought his overpowering strength.

You're aware of her vendetta against my family but continue to taunt us with her presence? Bauta asked. Tell me, what is your angle here Didanawisgi?

Make her my wife, Didanawisgi said and embraced her. When he kissed her the flames shot past his jaws and into her mouth to fill her skull.

17

James stood alone near the south rim of the Grand Canyon as the rising sun warmed the back of his stolen Carhartt. He rubbed his eyes with the palms of his hands and tried to forget about another restless night of lying on the ground in a sleeping bag meant for summer. When his exhaustion subsided he opened them to find layer after layer of orange, purple, red, yellow and brown rocks exposed by the Colorado River carving out what the Pueblos treated as a holy site. A shiver ran up his spine. He zipped up his coat and pulled a Chicago Bears hat over his disheveled brown hair.

What are you two doin? he asked the geriatric couple walking by but they kept at their errand without a word. They approached the edge and dropped their cheap bath robes to reveal their naked, wrinkled and sagging bodies with white hair in the appropriate places. They winced when the piercing wind cut through the paleolithic landscape and hit their exposed skin.

Son, we're returning to the Lord, the old man said and waved. And we hope you do the same when the time's right.

Please, dont be alarmed, the old woman said and smiled. We have nothing left to live for... our farm back in Illinois went up in flames... our kids are dead... so we've made our peace with God.

The old man embraced his wife, kissed her on the mouth and clasped her left hand in his right. They admired one another for the final time, gazed at the horizon and leaped into the chasm.

No, James screamed and ran to the edge but almost doubled over from his acrophobia. Their bodies bounced, heads cracked and limbs broke, leaving them in ridiculous positions. Their voices invaded his weary mind.

Down here James.

Join us James... join us.

He covered his ears in horror and scanned his surroundings but found no other witnesses. The sun was higher and the clear blue sky didnt mirror their archaic end. He peered over again as their lives spilled onto the rocks and trickled into the river.

Put an end to your suffering.

It's only natural to let go... so let go.

You cant save them James, let alone yourself.

With another peek he found dozens more suicides on the surrounding rocks being pecked at by crows. Pieces of flesh hung from their beaks. Their faces were wet from the suicides' blood. Their heads bobbed up and down but up long enough to stare at the unwelcome tourist and back to their breakfast.

There's no use in fighting the Fire.

Jump, jump, jump.

James? What are you doin? Jodie pleaded from where he stood

moments prior. She wore Rivera's bomber jacket and his dark blue hat with the FBI shield stitched into it. Her hands were stuffed in the pockets.

Mom, dont come over here, he said and picked up the bathrobes.

Who do those belong to?

You dont wanna know.

He stuck the robes under his arm and grabbed her by the elbow on the way to a bench sitting along the paved walkway. When they sat her expression scared him worse than the old couple's demise.

What were you doin so close to the edge? she asked.

I dont know if I'll ever forgive you Mom, he whispered without answering her questions. But until then I'm gonna fight to bring everyone back I wronged in Laredo.

You have to forgive me James, she pleaded but his mind was in another world. There's no other way to find peace for what I've put you through.

My friends... my Dad... Father O'Mally... I dont know if I'll ever be able.

James, it's time to go home now, she said as his energy shifted from innocent to dark. Let's grab Sheriff Dwyer and we'll leave all of this to the FBI... they'll track down the bald man and fix everything, I promise... it's time to go home now James... please, I cant lose you again.

I have to see this through.

But at what cost James? Your soul?

Mom, I'm goin to San Francisco with or without you and the rest of these people. He let go of the bathrobes and they floated along the breeze until falling into the canyon.

Just promise me one thing.

Sure.

Whatever you do... and wherever you go... do it with God... or you wont be any different than the people you're after.

They hurried back to the visitor's lot where the unmarked vehicles were parked side by side with the others waiting inside the cabs.

18

Come, come Morfran, Bauta yelled from his bedroom window as the afternoon sun cut through the low-hanging rainclouds over the roofs of the Lower Pacific Heights. He held out his wrinkled hand as a flock of crows passed by. One of the birds changed directions, glided back to the church and landed on his extended fingers. After retracting his arm he brought the bird close to his chest, latched the window and sat in his favorite chair. He put his feet up and stroked his feathered friend as they gazed into each others' eyes. It spun its greasy head toward the door and back to him, tilted it back and forth in quick succession and blinked several times.

The bitch is coming.

I know Morfran, he whispered as footsteps echoed down the hall.

You cant trust her Master... which means you cant trust Ohanzee either.

No need to worry, she's just a cog in the wheel... a wheel my weak-minded son will keep turning until we reach Italy.

They'll be sticking you in the catacombs if you dont keep your guard up Master.

You never lose your sense of humor, do you old friend? he asked it and chuckled.

There were three knocks on the door followed by the familiar clicking of the decagram handle and two cloaked individuals entered his bedroom. They bowed, lowered their hoods and folded their hands in anticipation of their Master's instructions but he continued to stroke his pet.

You summoned us Master? Ohanzee asked and caught his wife rolling her eyes at the devious old man.

Morfran explained to me that CK has been captured again, Bauta said by the window. He gave the crow a kiss on its head and waited until it rejoined the flock circling over the church before latching the window.

CK is a worthless fool, Angelica said. Why are we leaving the fate of Paytah and Yoki in his hands?

He has his uses, Bauta said.

I'm sorry Master, Ohanzee said and gave his wife a nasty glance.

CK will be on the Kern River tonight, Bauta said, pouring himself a glass of wine. If my crows dont return with the second volume, take your men to the redwoods tomorrow and retrieve it there.

Yes Master.

And use the desouling spell I taught you if his army wont submit to you.

What about me? Angelica asked.

You're staying here.

Why?

We need to test your congregation, Bauta retorted.

For what?

For faith of course.

The Sisters of Radiance have given up their families, possessions and futures to devote their lives to the Fire... what more could you possibly ask of them? she pleaded with a cracking voice and tears rolling down her cheeks.

The same thing I ask of all my followers... everything, Bauta said, stepping closer to the shaking woman.

Ohanzee and I have given you everything and we still dont have our children back, she said. Without notice a throbbing pain overwhelmed her womb.

I cant reflesh Paytah and Yoki until I have CK's book, Bauta said with a smile as the bald man glared at his wife writhing in pain. Besides, wasnt I the one who saved their souls after you burned them alive with one of your experiments?

I know... it was all my fault, she wept, tossing her head back and forth in agony.

Do everyone in this church a favor and simply obey me from now on, okay Sister Angelica?

Yes... yes I understand... please, let me go.

As you wish, Bauta said and released his grip on her soul.

You spoke out of place my love, Ohanzee whispered and put his arm around her. You disrespected our Master, so apologize... apologize now Angelica.

Apologize? she whispered and collected herself. You should be apologizing to me for allowing this... this deceitful old man to hurt me again and again.

Ohanzee, quiet your wife before I toss her out the window and have Morfran and his flock peck her to death, Bauta said and cackled as Angelica raised her hood and vacated the room in a fury.

19

Agent Munn, Sheriff Dwyer and Jodie stayed with the vehicles parked along a frontage road intersecting Highway 155. They were a quarter of a mile north of Agents Martinez and Rivera who stood on a rock formation halfway down the gorge surrounding the Kern River. With shotguns resting on their shoulders they kept an eye on every movement CK, James and Lauren made down by the water's edge. The cannibal sat on a boulder with the tattered volume in his hand while the farmboy and the blond sat across from him on a fallen tree. The southbound river had gone cold with the change of seasons and the mayflies and grasshoppers had disappeared with the tourists, trout fisherman and locals drinking beer, eating lunch and fucking in the bushes. It was a tranquil Monday except the cannibal's lesson shrouded the picturesque dusk in malevolence.

No, goddammit, CK said and winced as the cuffs around his wrists chained to the nearest pine clinked together. Listen farmboy, you aint gonna be able to use the Fire until you learn what you're sayin in Latin first, then you can conjure it up in your mind and make it come true, understand?

Well, they dont teach Latin at Laredo High School so give me a fuckin break, James said. He picked up a handful of rocks and tossed them into the Kern one at a time in frustration.

It's okay, try again, Lauren murmured and rubbed his back.

Come on, if you wanna get your stupid friends back you gotta keep tryin, CK said. He flipped to a different section without the teenagers noticing and studied the cursive written on the soiled page. The new spell rolled off his tongue with ease but before the farmboy could repeat the words the Master's crows descended on the gorge. They blacked out the sky with numbers somewhere in the thousands and cawed with such verbosity it was impossible to comprehend the cannibal's words. They dove and attacked the petrified teenagers to create a diversion.

Martinez, Rivera, help us, James yelled and tried to shelter Lauren but their talons scratched his arms and hands. Several clumps of her long hair were pulled from her scalp while he fought to keep them from plucking out her eyes.

Sorry farmboy, CK laughed, climbed back on the rocks and held the volume toward the sky as an offering. Two crows swooped down and yanked the book away but dropped several feet from its weight. After flapping their wings with abandon they generated enough power to clear the trees but successive shotgun blasts disintegrated them. The volume fell to the shore, opened and its pages fluttered in the wind as waves hit the rocks and sprayed water onto the cursive words and diagrams.

The book James, get the book, Martinez yelled. He shucked another round into the chamber of his twelve gauge and the double ought buck tore through the crows hovering above the teenagers. Two more blasts and the ground was covered in a feathery mess of flesh and guts.

I'll get it, Lauren yelled back. She fell to her hands and knees to avoid the other kamikazes and scurried across the rocks. Five landed on her back and drove their pointy beaks into her young skin but she managed to knock them off.

Get down, Rivera yelled at the cannibal and fixed his sights on his head. I said get the fuck down, now, now, now.

Okay, okay, CK said with both hands in the air, hopped off the rocks and laid on the ground. He faced west to stare at the blond nearing the water's edge and whispered in Latin. A six foot high wall of fire separated the girl and the book. It singed the ends of her hair but she extinguished it before the rest went up in flames.

Lauren, are you okay? James cried out. He ducked to avoid the last of the crows and ran to her side.

Fine, just get the book, Lauren yelled at him but the wall had doubled in size and intensity. The heat caused them to fall back from the firewall creeping toward the brush-covered riverbank.

You son of a bitch, Rivera screamed. He used the butt of his Remington to knock CK unconscious with a downward motion. The cannibal's head hit the rocky ground with a thud and a trickle of blood streamed onto the rocks. The crows abandoned their attack, returned to the sky and flew away without fulfilling their Master's orders as James and Lauren saved the volume from floating downstream.

20

On the morning of November 3rd the bald man led three of his servants into the sacristy, unlocked the hidden door and took the winding stairs past the catacombs. In the dungeon a fat guard with green and purple bruises on his face sat on a small wooden stool in the entryway picking his nails with a wavy dagger. When he couldnt make out the hooded guests he grabbed the torch jammed into the sconce on the wall and held it at arm's length.

How's Hong? Ohanzee asked and snatched it from his hand.

Depressed and irritable but he'll be happy to see you sir, the guard said, pulled a mess of keys from his pocket and found the correct one. I tried to feed him earlier this morning but he almost broke my nose 'cause I didnt bring him anything to drink.

Serves you right, Ohanzee chuckled. He followed him past the crowded cells holding a one-armed man, four crippled FBI Agents, conjoined twins, a half-dozen Sisters with their eyes removed, four midgets and a dozen young men who didnt work out as the Master's new servants. All wore tattered cloaks with the hoods lowered, filthy ropes tied arounds their waists and dirty bare feet. Their faces, hands and arms were burned in similar ways with boils, puss and blood oozing from their infected wounds. As the bald man and his company passed the repulsive prisoners reached out and begged to be set free but their pleas were disregarded by the callous men. When they reached the end of the hall they found a murky cell. Labored breaths came from a hooded giant sitting on the cot hanging from the wall by two chains.

Hong, you awake? Ohanzee asked and raised his torch to light the windowless quarters.

Yeah, I'm awake Anzee, Hong said with his deep and abrasive voice. He shook the floor to ceiling bars lumbering over to the bald man. The flames highlighted his face of boils.

Good, we have work to do, Ohanzee said, lit the sconce outside his cell and placed his left hand on the giant's.

I heard, what did CK do now?

It's what he didnt do.

Okay, what didnt he do?

He didnt bring the second volume back to our Master.

Sounds like CK's love of human flesh is crippling his judgement, Hong said and returned to his disgusting excuse for a bed. Watch out, here comes your better half.

You're taking Hong? Angelica asked with an old bottle of wine in her hand.

Of course I am, Ohanzee replied.

Hello Angie, Hong said.

Open this goddamn door, she demanded and the guard fumbled with the lock. Hurry, cant you see he's thirsty?

Yes ma'am, the guard said.

Out of the way, she said and handed him the bottle. My dear Hong, has the guard not been treating you well?

I could use more alcohol... other than that he treats me fine, why do you ask?

Because I want you to tell me if he's not, okay?

Sure.

Drink up, I need you to listen.

I'm listening, Hong said, tipped the bottle and streams of red trickled down his chin.

I want you to break my husband's neck if he doesnt return with CK's book, okay?

It would be my pleasure Angie but there's something I need.

And what's that?

I need new skin, Hong said and pulled back the left sleeve of his cloak. He grimaced in pain when her soft fingers cradled his arm so she could study his burns.

Hong, you agreed to let Master Bauta test his spells on you in exchange for your sins, did you not?

I'm fucking rotting to death down here Angie.

Hong, our Master caught you trying to take advantage of one of my Sisters, Angelica said as the prisoners in the adjoining cells crowded the dividing bars.

I know but I've paid for my sins many times over. Hong said, set the bottle down and rose to intimidate her. I'm getting tired of begging you.

Easy now Hong, Ohanzee said and tried to escort his wife to safety.

Master Bauta will burn you alive if you dont honor your end of the bargain, Angelica said and the giant wrapped his hands around her neck.

Stop it Hong, you're going to kill her, Ohanzee cried out as his servants came to his aid. Angelica was close to passing out as they tried to separate the two. The giant released his grip and his visitors fell against the stone wall in a tangled mess.

Fine... I'll get you out of here if you promise to come back with the book, deal? Angelica panted and raced out of the cell.

Deal, Hong said. He tipped back the half-empty wine bottle. He took three long gulps and let out a belch loud enough to excite the lingering prisoners.

You're a disgusting piece of shit Hong, Angelica said and he joined the others in laughter. Ohanzee, dont forget to take Master Bauta's sword just in case CK's army doesnt obey you.

21

The pink sun was breaking over the fields of produce when a white Ford van signaled to pass a northbound eighteen wheeler on Interstate 5 a few miles past the Highway 198 exit in Fresno County. A four-door cruiser of the same make and color duplicated the lane change at eighty miles an hour with three car lengths separating the two unmarked vehicles. Road-weary truckers, local farmers driving rusty old pickups and the occasional state trooper heading home after the late shift were the only traffic. A groggy and pissed Sheriff Dwyer was behind the wheel of the cruiser with Jodie wide awake in the passenger seat. In the back Lauren sat upright with her head resting against the window with Bob lying across her lap. He was snoring so loud the radio was worthless.

Up ahead in the van Agent Martinez took another sip from his insulated coffee mug as Agent Rivera slept in the passenger seat. CK was shackled to one of the parallel benches in the cargo bay with a wired Agent Munn keeping his twelve gauge pointed at him. James sat next to the agent with the book open in his lap following the cannibal's instructions. He was frustrated with his lack of ability to learn the spells but managed to keep his eyes open despite another night on the road.

That's it farmboy... you got it, CK whispered and became excited by the softball-sized flame hovering in the teenager's right palm. Keep repeatin the spell and let it grow now... let it grow.

Well I'll be goddamned, Munn said and lowered his weapon. The supernatural phenomenon painted oranges and yellows on their awestruck faces.

Quit talkin, I'm tryin to concentrate, James muttered without opening his eyes. The flame grew past his fingers and licked the ceiling. The cannibal and lawman sat back in their seats for fear he wouldnt be able to control his newfound power.

All right now, read the counter spell before you burn us up, CK said with great trepidation. Come on, read the other spell farmboy.

Except the flame kept growing and growing until it singed the right edge of the book, his jeans and even his eyebrows. When he reacted to the pain the flame engulfed the entire bay as the passengers tried to protect themselves. Martinez slammed on the brakes and overcompensated by spinning the wheel back and forth but the van darted across the highway, into the staging lane and spun around three times before hitting the graded shoulder. It slid for another twenty yards in the muddy field before coming to a complete stop parallel to the Gerald Ranch Airport. The windshield was cracked from Martinez's head colliding with it, the engine had quit and the others took several minutes to regain consciousness.

Martinez, are you okay? Rivera asked his partner. He pulled out his Leatherman tool and cut away his own seat belt. He propped himself up and put his index and middle fingers on his partner's neck but he still had a strong pulse. When he checked the bay Munn was in shock and the back doors were open.

What happened Rivera? Munn asked and reached for the chain snaked around the opposite bench. He held it up to show the agent the severed links still glowing red.

I'll find them, Rivera said.

He climbed out and drew his Glock as Dwyer backed down the shoulder of the interstate toward the van. After scanning the field he spotted James chasing after CK by the planes parked outside of the southernmost hangar. He sprinted across the two runways and flashed his badge at a middle-aged mechanic in overalls working on a crop duster. He raised his Glock, cleared the corners and found the cannibal reigning blows down on the farmboy in the middle of the concrete floor.

Put your hands up, Rivera shouted and set his sights on the back of CK's head.

Deus, mihi virtutem ignis hostes percussas, James yelled from his back and a flame shot from his hands. It threw the cannibal across the hangar where he hit the north wall and bounced onto the floor with a thud. The ensuing plume of smoke dissipated into the rafters but the cannibal groaned in pain as embers flew off his hair, beard and clothes.

I got him, Dwyer yelled at Rivera and recuffed him as Munn, Martinez and Jodie ran into the hangar.

What the hell happened? Jodie asked and knelt beside her son.

Looks like James figured out how to use the Fire... but he wasnt channeling Lucifer, that's for sure, CK said while the others stood in awe of the farmboy.

22

Good morning Master, Angelica crooned as one of her servants shut the rusty door leading to the exconjuratory of the bell tower. She pulled up her hood to protect herself from the elements and greeted the cloaked old man standing by one of the eight exposed windows. It was a misty afternoon in the Lower Pacific Heights but the Golden Gate Bridge was still visible from their vantage point. Miles away the eastbound and westbound traffic moved along at a steady pace and the seagulls flew to and from the architectural marvel with grace. A barge passed underneath the orange girders lined with flashing lights cutting through the thick fog. The slow vessel blasted its horn and the brutish soundwaves bounced off the choppy water, echoed around the bay and reached the bell tower before dissipating in their busy neighborhood.

It is, isn't it? Bauta replied without taking his eyes off the ships motoring out to the Pacific. Although I would love to see the sun shine at least once this fall.

You wanted to speak to me?

She stayed far down the corroded guard rail, using the iron pickets to anchor herself from wave after wave of his poisonous energy.

I most certainly do, he said and pulled a prepacked wooden pipe from his cloak. He used his body to shield the bowl from the breeze, snapped his fingers and a flame ignited the pungent tobacco. With a couple of puffs it glowed red and his smoky exhale drifted past her.

Master, I'm pleased to share with you that my congregation has enough members to resurrect Didanawisgi and his army when you so choose, she said. The makeup covering the bruise on the right side of her face caught his eye.

I hate to interrupt you Angelica but what is your eavesdropping servant's name? he asked while staring at the young girl trying to stay warm by the balcony door. She was pale skinned, without lipstick and her long red hair accentuated her skinny frame. Her eyes were a piercing blue.

Who, me? the servant asked and pointed at herself in confusion.

Yes, you, he said and took another toke off his pipe.

No need to worry about her Master, Angelia said.

I will be judge of that Angelica, he said, knocked his pipe on the wet guard rail to empty the bowl and gestured for her to join them. Come, come my child.

Yes, Master Bauta, how can I be of service to you? the servant answered with a proper southern accent. She raised her hood while walking over to them and kneeled.

Stand up and let me get a good look at you, he said and offered his hand. What is your name my child?

Stella, she whispered. Her palms began to sweat and a fiery

sickness permeated her senses as his eyes studied her from head to toe.

Where are you from Stella?

Louisiana... my grandpa owned a plantation in Vacherie.

And what brought you to the First Church of Radiance?

My family fell apart after daddy died... then we lost our land and my mother went crazy... my brother sent me here to find answers.

Answers to what?

What do you mean?

Answer me honestly my child, what were you seeking?

I... I wanted to know if my father went to heaven.

And what did you discover?

I dont know Master... I still dont know.

Sister Angelica, it seems we have a little problem here.

Stella, run along now, Master Bauta and I have much to discuss, Angelica interjected. Run along before you're reprimanded again.

Angelica, we have much to discuss but not like you mean, he said and offered his hand again. Please, take it my child... go on, take it.

Yes, Master, Stella said, clutching the wrinkled and veiny thing. She met his gaze as her eyes filled with dreadful tears.

Step up here, he said and tapped the ledge as Angelica's voice tiptoed into her servant's mind.

Just do what he says Stella, I wont let you fall.

Master Bauta?

Do not question him Stella.

Good my child, real good, he said while keeping ahold of her hand as she stepped onto the ledge. Stella, what you've been struggling with is a lack of faith.

Faith?

Yes, faith my child, and we're going to exercise your faith right now. When I let go, you will be on your own. If you believe in Sister Angelica's teachings, you will be able to balance on your own.

Master, please dont let go, I'm afraid of heights.

Dont show any weakness or he'll exploit it... please Stella, listen to me.

I'm letting go now Stella, he said but she wouldnt release her grip. Let go my child, just let go.

No, please, I'm going to fall, Stella cried out as the wind increased and the mist became rain. It blew through the openings, drenched their cloaks and puddles began to grow around their feet.

Master, she's just a girl, please dont do this to her, Angelica begged and extended her arms to brace the servant.

Stop, Angelica, another step and you will rob her of this experience. He let go of the servant's hand and grabbed the sleeve of the priestess' garb.

Oh my God, oh my God, Stella said and wobbled but caught herself on the rail.

No, do not use that, he shouted. I want you to stand on your own two feet without help from me or Sister Angelica.

Okay, Stella said and managed to steady herself with her eyes closed. I did it, I got over my fear of heights Master.

Good but now its time to open your eyes... go on now, he said and she did as instructed while extending her arms for balance. The rain was coming down in sheets and the wind made their cloaks flap with each gust.

Now take my hand, he said and a flame rose from his palm.

Master Bauta? Stella asked as it warmed her right side. It'll burn me, wont it?

What does your faith tell you?

I dont know.

Search your soul my child, do you believe in the Fire or do you still believe in fear?

I dont understand Master, please help me down.

Angelica, dont take another step, he said and pushed the priestess out of the way. Take my hand Stella, it will never burn if you live in faith. Please, take my hand... now.

Okay, Stella said. She stood tall and extended her right arm with great trepidation. When she went to cup the quivering flame her fingers told her neuroreceptors it was unsafe.

Believe in the Fire or I will push you over the railing you faithless little eavesdropper, he yelled and it rose to her eye level.

I will, I will, Stella swore and seized the flame. The stench of burning skin reached their nostrils. She let out a horrible cry and it climbed her arm and ignited her cloak.

Master, no, Angelica shouted as the servant's arms spun in circles. She slipped off the wet masonry and went over the brink in a thrashing blaze.

No, no, no, Stella cried out while doing a somersault in the air.

You son of a bitch, Angelica screamed at him and grabbed the vertical pickets as her servant hit the sidewalk. The fiery explosion was followed by a cloud of black smoke. Her burning remains were drowned by the storm. Lightening flashed over the bay and delayed thunder shook the exconjuratory.

Angelica, I asked you to groom women who are ready to hand their souls over to me before the great sacrifice, he said with no remorse for the smoldering corpse. Instead, you continue to enable their weaknesses.

But she was my... friend, Angelica gasped and covered her mouth in a feeble attempt to hide her disbelief. How could you do that after all I have done for you... and your son... and this horrible fucking church you two have imprisoned me in?

Clean that nosey brat off the sidewalk and I'll help get your congregation ready Angelica, Bauta said. He vanished through the access door, leaving the priestess alone to stare at Stella's blackened remains.

Cars and pedestrians making their way up and down Bush Street stopped in disbelief at the tragedy. A little old lady with purple hair and a clear umbrella stared at the distraught cloaked woman in the bell tower but walked away when a mysterious voice entered her feeble mind.

23

Servi Luciferum vocavi te Móyses et meam impleat praeceptum Domini iusiurandum remitti inferno supplicio, Ohanzee and his four servants chanted over and over again while holding hands in a circle near Stream Trail in Reinhardt Redwood Regional Park. The surrounding trees stood over three-hundred feet tall and cast the ferns, mosses, sorrell and trillium on the floor in shadow. Echoes of cracking limbs and trampled leaves reached their ears so they let go and formed an outward facing circle. The bald man adjusted the broadsword hanging from the rope tied around his waist as Hong and the three other servants became fearful of the surrounding evil. They searched in every direction with wide eyes and thumping hearts but there was no sign of CK's missing army.

Haec est ultima admonitio, he cried out but received no reply.

The crows perched on the branches above their heads went silent but focused their beady eyes at a clearing to the north. They sailed through the air for several seconds, landed above the source and pointed out the towering skeleton.

Ohanzee, the goliath called with a distorted voice.

I'm here... show yourself, he said and separated from his servants.

Where's CK? the goliath asked from behind the redwood.

He'll be not far from here later this evening, Ohanzee answered and motioned for the others to hold their positions. Please join us, time is of the essence.

No CK... no army.

We'll find him together but you have to trust me.

CK's our leader... not you, the goliath said and the crows took to the air and returned to the trees surrounding the bald man.

I'm your leader now.

No, you're not, the goliath said and skulked from behind the massive tree one hundred yards to the northeast. The eight foot tall creature showed no regard for anything in its path with its crushing long strides. Within seconds it covered twenty-five yards.

I order you to obey me, Ohanzee shouted. He placed his left hand on the metal scabbard and his right on the sword handle. Kneel and proclaim your allegiance to Master Bauta before I rip the Fire out of you.

Impossible, the goliath said and came to a stop twenty yards from him. The spaces between its left fibula and right ulna and radius bones were bridged with long rusty bolts.

I will.

Prove it, the goliath said with a creaking jaw missing the majority of its teeth. Barbed wire left over from the First World War was wrapped around its protruding ribs.

You're challenging Master Bauta's claim?

No, I challenge you.

You have an oath to fulfill to CK and CK swore an oath to Master Bauta and I am his next of kin, Ohanzee said, brandished the sword and drew a line in the mud. Cross this and I'll desoul you.

He whispered a spell in Latin and his servants confirmed the dark energy emanating from him. Their stomachs soured as the goliath took a step backward in dread.

24

What about Bobbio? Lauren asked while holding the farmboy's cold hand.

Don't worry, I'll figure out a way to heal him, James said. They walked along a sandy path leading to a reservoir where mallards gathered offshore. The flock bounced up and down on waves created by a sharp wind.

You promise? she asked when they slowed down beneath a cluster of live oaks but he didnt reply despite her flirtatious smile. Instead of embracing the blond he studied the approaching nimbostratus clouds as they rolled in from the west. Trails of rain pulled the dark gray from the bottom of the amorphous billows shadowing most of Merced County in autumn's gloom. The sun was fading as the purple needle grass swayed without rhythm.

Its gonna rain any minute, he said, let go of her hand and something pulled his attention toward the mallards. My dad and I used to duck hunt back home. I shot one last fall and had to carry it back to the truck in the pocket of my jacket.

That's gross and still you didnt answer my question farmboy. She blocked his view of the lake with her curvy figure but failed to hold back her pain. Her body trembled and she had trouble finding the right words.

What did you ask me? he asked and met her gaze.

Do you promise to help my father? she whispered. He put his hands on her hips and stared into her hazel eyes.

Yeah... I promise, he whispered. Her soft and feminine body warmed his hands. His hormones responded to her arms around his neck. He wanted to cover up the bulge under his jeans but she pressed herself against his skinny frame.

I've been wanting to kiss you since we picked you up in Missouri, she whispered. They both needed to brush their teeth and shower but neither cared about those superficial things. Their first kiss was awkward and noisy and their hearts raced and their hands explored each others' necks, chests and asses.

Did you hear that? he asked as the night pushed the sun past the meridian. The stars were hiding behind the approaching bank of storm clouds and the moon was in Pisces.

It's just the ducks farmboy, she said as the southbound flock congregated into a V-shape over their heads.

Oh fuck, he said and pushed her out of his view. They're here.

Who? she asked and squinted her eyes as a skeleton breached the surface of the rippling lake.

The drenched creature struggled to walk through the mud and muck of the shore. Another came out of the water and two, five and twelve more emerged from the depths. One by one the flames in their eyes lit up the shore, sandy beach and hiking path leaving the young lovers in a state of shock.

Run, he yelled, grabbed her hand and pulled her away from the fast approaching horde of former rapists, killers and thieves. They sprinted down the trail and to the parking lot as the creatures closed the distance. Agents Martinez and Rivera were working under the hood of the van while Munn pointed a Maglite at the overheated engine. Dwyer and Jodie walked up with their own flashlights and shined them on the panicked teenagers.

Where the fuck were you two? Dwyer asked. He raised both hands in the air and dropped them in frustration.

James, I'm gonna wring your skinny neck, Jodie said and shined her Maglite in their eyes.

They're right behind us, Lauren yelled and they caught dozens of flaming eyes bouncing up and down.

Martinez, Rivera, fuck this engine, we gotta go, Munn said and the agents piled into the van where CK slept in the cargo bay.

Oh fuck, Jodie said and opened the passenger door of the cruiser. The teenagers piled onto either side of Bob.

Dwyer threw it in reverse and checked the rearview mirror as the skeletons reached for the squealing vehicles. Rain began to fall on the **SAN LUIS RESERVOIR RECREATION AREA** sign at the end of the asphalt. They picked up speed on Basalt Road, slowed before the underpass and swerved onto the Interstate 5 north ramp.

25

Thank you for joining me on this dreary afternoon my beloved Sisters, Bauta said from behind the wooden pulpit. Lightening flashed through the stained-glass windows and the chandeliers sputtered as the cathedral lost power. Angelica was sitting in one of the three chairs before the high altar and he gazed at her for several moments. When the priestess caught on she stood and directed her servants to light the votive candles. As the storm raged outside the nave was filled with the same natural light intended by the original architects.

Pardon the interruption my Sisters but even I cannot control the weather, Bauta said as the servants returned to their pews. Now, if Angelica can lower the decagram we can begin the ceremony.

The priestess walked over to the ambulatory and untied the silver rope looped around the fastener situated on the wall. She used both hands to lower the decagram mirror hanging from the vault until it was several inches from the marble floor. The congregation smiled and giggled when they caught their reflections between the diagonal lines of the circular frame cast in silver.

Repeat after me, Bauta said and raised his hands. Omnipotens Lucifer, autem voco intra portas aperire ad decagram magistris.

After three repetitions it transformed from mirroring the female congregation to a deep red to a Roman cathedral. Four cloaked figures stood in a cluster wearing silver masks.

Sisters, meet the Circle of Fire, Bauta said as the congregation bowed to the ominous figures. Masters Pulcinella, Moretta, Brighella and Gnaga, meet the First Church of Radiance.

You promised to heal me, a woman cried out and stopped the introductions cold.

Who dares to speak now? Angelica asked, searching the crowd. Please, come forward and reveal yourself.

I gave up my hometown, my family, my friends to come here, the woman said. From the back of the cathedral an Indian woman in her late fifties used all of her upper body strength to set her squeaking wheelchair in motion. She was halfway down the nave before the priestess took the altar stairs.

Angelica, let her be, Bauta boomed while catching up to her. Come my child, come and state your case.

I've devoted the last twenty years of my life to this godforsaken church, the woman said, reached the end of the pews and stopped. And I'm just as crippled as the day I joined.

Diya, watch your mouth, Angelica said and grabbed her wheelchair handles. We don't speak to Master Bauta or any of the Masters that way. Apologize at once or be punished.

Stop, Angelica, I said let her be, Bauta said and kneeled to meet her gaze. Tell me Diya, have you been utilizing Sister Angelica's teachings in your life?

Yes, every day, Diya said, falling under his hypnotic spell.

And you're praying?

Every chance I get.

Good, good... but let me ask you something, do you believe?

Believe in what?

The Fire, what else are we here for?

Of course I do, what kind of question is that?

The only question that matters, he said and motioned to his servants waiting in the sacristy. Gentlemen, will you please escort Diya over to the mirror?

Master? she asked and was alarmed by the burn victims walking down the altar stairs.

Dont worry, they may look unwell... but they're strong, Bauta said chuckling as they cradled her in their arms.

Why are you doing this Master? Why are you entertaining my skepticism? she asked.

Quiet my child, Bauta said following the servants up the stairs. My dear Master Pulcinella, please show this poor woman the meaning of faith.

Of course, Pulcinella said. He extended his right arm to break the barrier and opened his hand. With a whisper of Latin and the twirling of his fingers a flame rose from his palm inches from her face. The magic reflected in her eyes.

Diya, show me you truly, truly believe in the Fire and take it from Master Pulcinella, Bauta said while her arms and feet dangled from the servants' arms.

No, it'll burn me, she said and recoiled in fear.

Diya, do you want to walk again?

Yes, of course I do but not this way, she said without taking her eyes off Pulcinella's hand.

Then believe with all of your heart... reach out and take it.

I believe, she said but retracted her arm when her nerves warned her fingers about the coming pain.

Do it, or you will live the rest of your days in that disgusting excuse for a wheelchair.

I believe Master Bauta, I believe.

Do it now, or I will expel you from this congregation, Bauta yelled. She closed her eyes out of frustration and wrapped her shaking hand around the flame even though it blistered her skin.

Good, now pull it out of his hand, he said and she brought it to her bosom. Keep your eyes shut and imagine your flesh absorbing the Fire... flowing through your veins... and into your heart.

Her palm absorbed the flame and a flickering light under her skin worked its way to her wrist. It glowed bright enough beneath her cloak to be visible when it reached her shoulder and chest. She spasmed for several seconds when it settled in her heart and the congregation oohed and awed at the phenomenon.

We need to call an ambulance, a brunette in the back pew shouted and put her hands on her face in shock. She's having a seizure.

You're killing her, a redhead in the front row cried out as the servants witnessed the handicap's vascular system distribute the Fire to every part of her body. After several moments she opened her eyes.

Don't you dare do a thing, Bauta said to the women. Diya, are you ready to walk now?

Yes, I'm ready, she said with profound hope.

You tell me, he said and the servants set her down.

Her weakness became strength and her toes and feet and calves and knees and hips responded with balance. Without warning the Master and his servants stepped away and she was left alone, rocking back and forth while reaching out for help but received none. After several near falls she remained steady as the congregation applauded their Sister's miraculous transformation.

26

Luciferum... vocavi te veniet de igne spoliare possit absorbere... sceleton anima, Ohanzee chanted while trying to pull the flames from the skeleton's chest by motioning with his hands from a safe distance. The goliath tried to run but the bald man's grip on its soul was too tight so it knocked him to the soaking ground with the back of its fleshless hand. He managed to draw his Master's sword before it attacked again and whispered a spell in Latin as quick as it would roll of his tongue. Starting at the cross guard a flame grew, ran down the fuller and ended at the point. He swung the fire sword from the three o'clock to the nine o'clock position to slice through its left knee. The goliath clenched its femur and howled loud enough to send the staring crows to safer branches.

Anzee? Hong cried out as the henchmen surrounded the fight. They checked over their shoulders as the rest of CK's army crept closer and closer.

Stay back or they'll never obey me, he said, using all of his might to cut through the goliath's other leg near its hip. It fell backward, thrashing and reaching the way turtles do when they're flipped onto their shells. He raised the flaming blade toward the night and brought it down on its left shoulder. The separated arm clawed its way toward Hong but lost its power after several seconds. Once, twice and on the third heave the bald man cut through the rusty barbed wire holding together its mangled rib cage. The two halves sprang open and flames shot onto its face, hands and cloak. He dropped his father's sword and tossed the burning fabric aside to reveal the 9mm harness running around his left shoulder and across his chest.

When he repeated the spell the fires in the goliath's eyes crept down its spine and joined its blazing chest where a silhouette of Phoebe danced inside the flames. He couldnt turn away from the prophecy. Moments passed as the winged skeleton crawled from the wreckage of his wife's church, faced him and howled inside his mind.

Snap out of it Anzee, it's trying to trick you, Hong yelled.

The silhouette lost its control over him as he repeated the spell in rapid succession. When he could no longer take the pain he reached past the wire and splintered ribs and into the flames. The unbearable temperature told him to retreat but he found the strength to pull the Fire out and into the air. The goliath let out one last scream as its centuries old bones scattered onto the ground.

Ohanzee, Hong yelled, raised his fists and the other henchmen caught on as they celebrated their leader's victory. They kept chanting his name and lowered their hoods and reached for the flames to sample the stolen power.

Stay back, Ohanzee cried out as his boiling and blistering hands tried to contain the unrelenting flames. After several moments his fingers and palms managed to absorb it and a plume of black smoke rose into the air, leaving the party under the darkness of the forest canopy. Rain drops did little to sooth his burnt legs, crotch and chest as he studied the goliath's remains.

Do you hear that Anzee? Hong asked who was triggered by the movements in all directions. They're still out there.

They've surrounded us, Ohanzee whispered. He picked up and sheathed the sword while searching for the hidden army. Ready yourselves, they might attack.

His servants did as they were told and a scourge of footsteps filled the redwoods until the skeletons formed a hundred yard wide circle. The bald man staggered past his men stark naked. He had lost most of his pubic hair and his arms and legs were riddled with first-degree burns.

Come out, come out wherever you are, Ohanzee whispered. The youngest and most untrained of his servants offered his cloak. He pulled it over his tender body. A lone owl hooted overhead on a branch large enough to put most pine trees to shame.

They're everywhere, Hong whispered in-between gasps. I can feel them... my stomach's on fire.

Dont let them overpower you, Ohanzee said. He concentrated on a clearing where the rising moon cut through the trees and high-lighted a faction of the creatures. There were dozens of them in all different shapes and sizes without flames in their eyes or ribs.

Leader, one of the paleolithic skeletons whispered with a tortured voice but the rest remained motionless. The moonlight empha-sized their skulls, clavicles and spines with accents on their jagged bones. Their chests moved in and out with the memory of still living but their jaws created no clouds of breath.

Come out... all of you, Ohanzee said and waited. The night was coming on strong and clear and the stars were revealing them-selves up in the heavens.

Our new leader, the skeleton said and twin flames appeared in every direction. Most in groups, others alone and some within yards of the defeated goliath.

Yes... I am Ohanzee... your new leader... and I will fulfill the oath that CK made to our Master, he said and approached it. Dont worry... your souls are safe with me until we reach Master Bauta.

Ohanzee, the skeleton said again and again in jagged syllables until the entire army caught on. The chant filled the redwoods with malicious energy, killing animals for a mile in every direction.

27

It was almost pitch dark when Agents Martinez and Rivera poached a white-tailed deer at Reinhardt Redwood Regional Park. They used the scoped Winchester 30-06 borrowed from the trunk of Munn's cruiser to hit it in the hindquarters from a quarter mile. After they clicked on their Maglites they tracked the hobbling ten point buck along Stream Trail for a hundred yards and found it lying on the bank of Redwoods Creek. It was trying to lap up the frigid water when it spotted their approach. Blood trickled from its mouth and the wound on its back left hip changed its brown fur to maroon. Martinez slung the rifle over his shoulder as Rivera dropped his right knee onto its ribs and pulled two large plastic zip ties from his jacket. They strapped it to a log and carried it on their shoulders back to their campsite hidden among the gigantic trees.

Lay it on that one, CK said and pointed with handcuffs around his wrists to one of the two six foot wide pentagrams he was sculpting on the ground out of rocks. Okay, tie it down.

I got it, James said as he finished sharpening the last of twelve stakes cut from green branches with Rivera's multi-tool. He fed them through its bound hooves and used a flat stone to hammer them into the soggy ground.

CK, you act like you've done this a million times, Munn said standing beside Dwyer with shotguns propped on their hips.

Munny Bunny, I've done things you'd never dream of, he said without facing the agent.

Better hope it works or I'm gonna cut your balls off since none of these guys were man enough to do it back in Texas, Lauren said. She sat next to Jodie on the blanket spread out for Bob close to the campfire. He was fast asleep and snoring from the last of Dwyer's bottle of painkillers.

Easy young lady, we're all friends now, CK said while hobbling over to the terrified buck.

The hell we are, Lauren said, stood and stole the tool from James. After what you did you're lucky to be alive you sick fuck.

Lauren, give me that goddamn thing, James said and stole it back. If we dont listen to CK we might lose Bobbio.

The farmboy's right, so how about somebody carry him onto the other pentagram before this deer croaks? CK asked.

Martinez, Rivera, get to it, Munn said and moved the shotgun to his other hip. The young agents used the blanket underneath Bob to lift and carry him over to the unoccupied bed of organized rocks but hurried away as if the unholy symbol was poisonous. James pulled the volume from his jacket, handed it to the cannibal and waited with the others in quiet desperation.

Now I want five of y'all to stand around Bobbio, join hands and repeat after me, CK said. He opened the jagged pages of the old book to the refleshing spell.

Come on people, we aint got all night, Dwyer said. He shucked the slide on his shotgun back and checked the magazine.

You got one opportunity to make this work CK or I'm cuttin you down with this double ought buck, you hear me? Munn asked.

Oh, I hear you Munny Bunny.

Martinez, Rivera, James, Lauren and Jodie stood at the five apexes. They were cold, tired and scared out of their minds as the cannibal read the spell in Latin. By the third repetition they were in synch as the damp wind quit and their energies shifted from unnerving to poisonous. Their minds reeled and Lauren wanted to puke up what little food was in her stomach but kept it down by staring at her despondent father.

Whatever you do, dont stop, CK said and placed his left hand on the deer's heart while holding the book in his right. It bucked against the stakes but was unable to break free as its bloodstained fur began to smolder and little flames emerged around the cannibal's black fingers. After another repetition of the ancient words he pulled its Fire away without it burning his palm. He closed the book, walked over to Bob's pentagram and knelt between Martinez and Rivera.

What the fuck are you doing to him? Munn exclaimed and leveled the shotgun. Answer me, now.

Just stay back you damn fool, CK yelled and Dwyer grabbed the agent's shoulder. All right people, you can stop chantin now. Lauren, pull that blanket off Bobbio.

She obeyed as the others gathered around hoping her father would spring to life from his pain and suffering but his breaths had gone shallow. His eyes were twitching while he mumbled something about his dead wife and sons back in Indiana.

Stay strong Bobbio, this'll all be over soon, Lauren said. She knelt beside him and cradled his hand.

Y'all might wanna brace yourselves, CK said and placed his flaming hand on Bob's exposed shoulder. The burning flesh gave off a terrible stench causing the bystanders to cover their noses and mouths with their shirts and jackets.

Did it work? Jodie asked and crowded around Lauren for a better view of the miracle.

You bet your white ass it did, CK said.

He removed his hand and after several moments Bob's mangled flesh absorbed the flame. The lacerations festered as the Fire re-built his ligaments, muscles and skin. It glowed and sizzled until tender scar tissue took the place of the rotting wound. Lauren cried tears of joy.

28

The hands on Agent Munn's wristwatch read 7:37pm when the moon hung atop the November sky. It hung there without a cloud to interfere with it casting the redwoods in dark blue. Martinez and Rivera hauled pine needles, branches and logs back to their campsite and stoked the fire to warm everyone's aching bones. Lauren and Jodie heated up three family-sized cans of chicken noodle soup in a cast iron pot and served it with the plastic bowls and utensils they purchased back in Gustine. They sat cross-legged on the wool blankets Sheriff Dwyer found in the van and stared past the flames as they ate in silence. CK set his bowl down and laid back to shut his eyes as James walked over to the picnic table, picked up one of the shotguns and pointed it at the cannibal.

What the fuck are you doin? Jodie asked and dropped her soup bowl on the ground and raised her hands.

Dont you point that thing toward Bobbio, Lauren said and used her body to cover him from any possible crossfire. He moaned but didnt wake from her weight.

Martinez, Rivera, you know the drill, Munn said with noodles in his mouth. The agents rose and brandished their sidearms. They went slow and easy with no intention of firing while managing to flank the farmboy.

Tie him down, James whispered as the campfire highlighted the Remington's barrel. Tie him down or I'll blow his head off.

That's not gonna happen farmboy, so why dont you tell me what your plan is? Munn asked. He set his bowl down with the hope of eating it later and stood while drawing his Glock.

Put your gun down Munn, Dwyer said as he waved his hands.

Don't you dare point your weapons at my son, Jodie said and stood in front of him. I swear to God, if you shoot him I'll kill all three of you with my bare hands.

Get the fuck outta the way Jodie, Munn barked, motioning with his pistol. I didnt trek half-way across the United States to lose the Campground Killer to your crazy son.

CK's taught me everything I need to know about bringin my friends and family back, so let's get started, James said without taking his eyes off the prisoner.

Oh, this is gettin good, CK chuckled and laid back on his blanket to take in the sky.

Shut up CK, Munn said without the iron sights on his pistol leaving their target. James, how on God's green Earth do you plan on doing that?

We start by using CK to bring my dad back from Hell, James said. He flicked the safety off and put his finger on the trigger.

You got my approval, Lauren said and checked her father's pulse on his neck. Far as I'm concerned, CK's fair game for what he did to Bobbio.

Talk to me kid, what can we do to change your mind? Munn asked.

There's nothin to talk about, James said and the weapon became heavy in his arms. Then we can use that bald motherfucker that torched Laredo and the rest of those evil bastards out in San Francisco to get my buddies and Father O'Mally back.

An eye for an eye, right CK? Lauren asked and made sure the blanket was covering her father's shoulders.

Dont drag me into this girl, CK said with a beaten voice. Far as I'm concerned the farmboy aint ready quite yet.

Agent Munn, I obviously know James better than anyone here and he's not bluffin, Jodie said and lowered her arms. Better do what he says 'cause CK's gonna die either way.

All right James, have it your way, Munn said. He holstered his Glock as the waning fire chewed through a thick log. It spat out black and gray smoke carrying orange sparks above their camp.

Boss? Rivera asked without lowering his pistol.

Yeah, we cant let you do that Boss, Martinez confirmed without compromising his position.

You can and you will boys, Munn said, gesturing for them to stand down. The world we knew even a few months ago has changed, so we're gonna have to change with it.

You cant be serious, Martinez asked.

I'm dead serious... but if James fucks up, I'll take the rap, Munn said to the sheriff.

Ditto, Dwyer said.

Y'all gonna let the farmboy experiment on me? CK asked.

Sorry CK but it's time to pay the piper, Dwyer said and struck the prisoner on the back of the head with the butt of his revolver. He grabbed his military jacket and dragged him over to the stony pentagram they had used for Bob.

Martinez, Rivera, tie him down, Munn commanded.

Thank you Agent Munn, James said. He set the shotgun down and grabbed the book off the picnic table. After he ran his fingers over its cover sickness filled his stomach.

You sure you know what you're doin? Jodie whispered.

No but what choice do we have? James asked and thumbed through the pages.

All right, he's ready, Martinez reported and stepped away from the pentagram to reveal the cannibal lying on the stones with his arms and legs tied to the stakes. His eyes were closed and his breaths hung in the air.

Make sure he suffers for what he did to Bobbio, would you? For me? Lauren asked the farmboy.

I dont wanna kill anybody, let alone make them suffer, James whispered and caught the surprise in her face.

I'm sorry... I didnt mean to make this any harder on you, Lauren breathed in his ear.

It's okay, I know what you meant, James whispered and kissed her rosy cheek. All right, I need five volunteers.

Martinez, Rivera, you heard him, Munn said and threw another log on the fire.

I'm in, Jodie said and made her way over to the pentagram.

Same here, Dwyer said and grabbed her hand.

I guess that leaves me, Lauren said and stood near the last apex.

Good, now repeat after me, James said and angled the book to catch the firelight.

Stop, a man yelled and the echoing word caused the campers to break hands. They turned around in circles and stared into the dark hoping to find someone playing a prank but a barrage of footsteps proved otherwise. With each passing moment sickness permeated their senses and the chicken noodle soup gurgled in their bowels.

Who's out there? Munn asked and pointed his pistol into the dark without a reply. Martinez, Rivera, grab those shotguns.

You got it Boss, Martinez said as they took defensive positions behind the nearest redwoods, pointing the weapons toward the snapping twigs.

Show yourself, Dwyer yelled but the waiting game continued as the campfire burned brighter than it had all evening. It was pitch black twenty feet past their site. Nothing moved except the clouds rolling in from the west as they blanketed the stars and moon.

We're coming out, the man said and confident footsteps advanced from the south.

Wait... dont shoot... I know that voice, Dwyer cried out as the firelight outlined their hooded cloaks. The sheriff's heart almost exploded when he caught a glimpse of the bald man's face.

And I remember yours, Ohanzee said with his three servants and Hong at his back.

Son of a bitch, Dwyer said and cocked his stainless steel Ruger. Dont come any closer or I'll finish what I started back in Laredo.

There's no need for violence Sheriff, Ohanzee said and smiled. But it'll be a bloody night if you dont hand CK, James and Lauren and the second volume over.

Not a chance, Munn said with his sights on the bald man as he signaled for the army of skeletons to ignite their empty cavities.

They're fuckin everywhere, James said and stood in front of Lauren as dozens of twin flames revealed their numbers. There were two goliaths and close to a hundred adult, teenage and child-sized skeletons lurking amongst the redwoods.

Do as I say, or I'll sick my Master's army on you, Ohanzee said.

Dont you mean my army? CK asked, lifting his concussed head off the ground.

I'm sorry old friend, I promise to make it up to you, Ohanzee said and nodded.

You bald motherfucker, CK whispered.

I said turn over CK, James and Lauren and the second volume,

Ohanzee yelled at the campers.

No, James said. He stuck the second volume in his Carhartt and shot fire from his hands. It traveled across the camp and struck the bald man's borrowed cloak and his left side ignited but he managed to pat out the flames before his skin endured more abuse. He drew the Glock 9mm from his shoulder harness, aimed it at Jodie and squeezed the trigger.

Mom, James screamed and caught her in his arms but her eyes had already rolled into the back of her head. Blood was leaking from the corners of her mouth and the gaping wound in her chest painted his left hand red.

Bring them to me, Ohanzee said as he holstered his pistol. The two goliaths advanced on the camp while the rest of the army remained in the dark.

Fire, Munn screamed and fired six hallow points from his Glock at the goliath missing the top half of its skull.

Martinez and Rivera unloaded round after round from their Remington's. Each shot knocked it off balance and damaged its armor-covered bones but it still found the agents hiding behind the massive trees. It reached down and pulled Munn out by his left ankle and stomped on his chest to render him unconscious. After it seized Martinez by his neck it took several steps and did the same to Rivera. The goliath hoisted their thrashing bodies into the air, paused and smashed their skulls together three times. When they fell limp it tossed them on the ground to search for the farmboy.

With no regard for the gunfire coming from the sheriff the goliath with an iron arm ripped CK from the improvised stakes and threw him over its right shoulder. It carried him to the blanket closest to the campfire where Lauren was draped over Bob in hopes of protecting him from the chaos. It ripped the blond from her father, tossed her onto its free shoulder and trampled through the flames and past the approaching bald man. Ohanzee put his muddy foot on Bob's throat and smiled at the farmboy paralyzed by his mother's death. With all of his weight he smashed Bob's larynx.

Baldy, Dwyer yelled across the camp but the half-skulled goliath intercepted his first shot with its massive hand. The second removed part of its mandible as he galloped closer and the third went through its spine. When the goliath was six feet away it slapped the revolver from his hands and threw him across the camp. He bounced off the tree closest to the farmboy and tumbled to the ground as the canopy spun clockwise in his smoke-filled eyes.

Stop, James yelled and glared at the bald man with his arms extended and palms facing out. I'm beggin you to stop.

Stop? Ohanzee asked as his servants circled the farmboy. We didnt even need to start if you would've heeded my warnings and didnt come looking for me. Now surrender the book or die.

Never, James said and the half-skulled goliath descended on him. It snatched the farmboy's right arm, hoisted him to eye level and ripped the second volume from his jacket.

Careful, our Master wont be pleased if it's ruined, Ohanzee said and motioned for it.

The goliath did as it was told but James knocked the goliath, bald man, his servants and the giant to their backs with an uncontrolled explosion. The fire caught the surrounding ground cover, bushes and tree trunks on fire. Before the bald man could regain the upper hand the farmboy crawled over to the sheriff and raised an impenetrable firewall.

Leave them, I've got the book, Ohanzee said as the goliath yanked him to his feet. Just grab the FBI agent and let's get the fuck out of here.

·

29

The winding stairwell under the First Church of Radiance went past the catacombs and dungeon and ended at a pair of twelve foot tall iron doors responsible for keeping the Christian world from the cavern. On the other side a worn trail cut through a maze of stalagmites leading to irregular stairs carved into a rock formation with a landing stretched across its top. On the west end were two six foot wide silver decagrams on stands bolted to the earth and on the east end Master Bauta and Angelica stood behind a pulpit carved from onyx. The flame atop his staff illuminated the servants below who were using hammers, picks and shovels to carve a pentagram into the limestone floor cleared of stalagmites. Their raucous work halted when marching engulfed the east tunnel.

Come my child, we have been waiting your return, Bauta yelled as the bald man emerged from the opening with an improvised torch in hand.

Good morning Master Bauta, Ohanzee yelled back as he led his servants, Hong, CK, Agent Munn, Lauren and the line of skeletons into the cavern. Once the Master's servants dropped their tools and retreated to the north and south walls the creatures marched onto the petroglyph, knelt and lowered their skulls. All were missing bones but their handmade metal armor, splints and

155

prosthetics made each one unique.

I see you left the other virgin in the redwoods, Bauta said while Angelica scowled at her husband.

I'm sorry Master, the farmboy's learning how to use the Fire quicker than anticipated, Ohanzee said without raising his head.

And how many times was your cannibal friend apprehended crossing the United States? Bauta asked as he rapped his unkempt fingernails on his staff.

I'm sorry Master, I had no control over my addiction, CK muttered and opened his arms. I may be injured now but my faith in the Fire has never been stronger. I'm sane again. Please, you gotta believe me Master.

Silence, Bauta yelled and banged his staff on the landing. You have failed me time and time again. For your recklessness I am taking control of your army until I find a use for you.

But Master, what about our deal? CK said with tears in his swollen eyes as the bald man's servants surrounded the cannibal.

The deal was for you to fetch the second volume and the skeletons in the Midwest without interference from the law, Bauta said as his staff burned taller. In addition, you delayed Didanawisgi's arrival and the refleshing of Paytah and Yoki.

Ohanzee, Sister Angelica, I'm sorry, CK said and dropped to his knees with his hands clasped. I'm beggin you, please hear me out for your own safety. The second book is too strong, it will consume you like it consumed me.

Hong, take CK and Agent Munn to the dungeon at once, Bauta

said and gestured toward the cavern doors. Go now before I order you to cut off his head.

Anything you say Master, Hong said and grabbed the cannibal and agent by the backs of their jackets. He hauled them down the trail as they kicked and screamed for clemency.

Ohanzee, I commend your patience with CK but he cannot be trusted, Bauta said once they were out of view.

I'm sorry my loyalty to him disrupted your plans, Ohanzee said. He closed his eyes and shook his head in disgrace.

Enough with the cannibal already, bring me the second volume my child, Bauta said and the bald man climbed the embankment stairs. Now let's transport these skeletons to Italy before the other Masters lose their trust in the First Church of Radiance.

30

Sheriff Dwyer parked the Ford on East 15th Street in the San Antonio neighborhood of Oakland and shut down the clanking engine. The windshield wipers were stuck in the three o'clock position, mud was caked around the wheel wells and the cabin stunk of burning oil from escaping the redwoods. He dropped his head onto the steering wheel and closed his eyes. James sat grieving in the passenger seat. Not only were they physically exhausted from the conflict on Wednesday night but mentally disturbed from digging shallow graves for Jodie, Bob and Agents Martinez and Rivera. The sheriff lifted his weary head and peered through the dirty windshield. Two old nuns stood on the front stairs of the church across the street beckoning the travelers. They approached the holy women with caution but were told to read the replaceable letter sign situated near the sidewalk.

SAINT MICHAELS CATHOLIC CHURCH
FATHER OMALLY
DAILY MASSES 9AM & 5PM
SATURDAYS 5PM
SUNDAYS 10AM & 5PM

This cant be, James said and stuck his hands in his pockets.

What?

This is the same sign as my church back home... same priest... even the same dates and mass times.

Are you sure?

I'm positive.

It's probably just a coincidence.

No, something drew us here... cant you feel it?

Come on, let's get back in the car and figure out what we're gonna do next, Dwyer said but the farmboy walked inside. He followed him, stuck his hand in the stoop and made the invisible sign of the cross over his forehead, chest and each shoulder. After walking down the nave he spotted the farmboy on the right section of pews and scooted down the third isle and lowered the kneeler. While studying the ceiling, altar and stations of the cross on either wall he noticed a trace of smoke leftover from the morning's mass.

Father O'Mally? James asked and stood in awe of the weathered priest walking down the altar stairs. Is that really you?

Yeah, it's me, James, O'Mally answered. He hung his arm over the pew to face them. The middle-aged Irishman's hair was still salt and pepper, face wrinkled and eyes piercing blue.

You died in that old farmhouse... outside of Laredo, Dwyer said in a state of shock. Everybody in Stratford County knows you're dead... how can you be here?

Are you a ghost? James asked.

Sit down and I'll explain everything, O'Mally said, put his hand on the farmboy's and smiled as they returned to the uncomfortable bench. I only have a little bit of time before this connection is lost.

Connection? Dwyer asked but the priest waved his hand in the air.

Sheriff, just shut the hell up and listen, O'Mally said and took a deep breath. James, how you use the Fire in this life will determine where you end up in the afterlife. If you use it to serve God, you will go to Heaven. If you use it to serve Lucifer, you will go to Hell, do you understand?

Yeah... but I tried using it to save my buddies back home and failed, James said. I tried using it again in the redwoods to save my mom and my new friends and failed again... what am I doing wrong Father?

You already said it, you're failing, O'Mally said and began walking up the altar stairs. God didnt give us the power to manifest our souls into a physical form like the fire just to fail. You must succeed in order to stop what's coming.

And what's comin? Dwyer asked.

The Permanent Halloween, O'Mally said and disappeared into the sacristy.

The what? Father, where are you goin? James asked, jumped over the pew and ran up the stairs as Dwyer sat contemplating the paranormal encounter. Father, where are you? I have so many questions, come back, I need to know if my dad is with you, please, it's driving me crazy, are my buddies with you?

After they searched for the priest but found no one in the church or rectory so they went outside. Cold had blanketed the neighbor-hood and the sky had grown purplish gray. A light mist covered their faces. The telephone lines running from the southeast corner of the church to the street poles were littered with noisy crows. They cawed at them and jockeyed for the best position on the slack metal wires. The sheriff zipped up his heavy jacket, checked the clasp on his gun holster and coughed loud enough to startle the crows. James walked back over to the sign, crouched down and studied the changes.

SAINT NICHOLAS CATHOLIC CHURCH
FATHER OSULLIVAN
DAILY MASSES 9AM & 5PM
SATURDAYS 5PM
SUNDAYS 10AM & 5PM

Can I help you? an Irish priest with a white beard asked from behind the cracked front door. He had a puzzled expression on his face and seemed to be scared of the road worn travelers.

Sir, what's your name? Dwyer asked and removed his hat.

Father O'Sullivan, this is my church, why? he asked and opened the door a little wider. They ran back to the cruiser and sped away before making formal introductions.

31

Where are you taking us? Lauren cried out as Hong dragged her and Agent Munn by a chain running through their shackles past the cells full of prisoners. There were more burn victims from the Master's experiments, local cops and a few battered FBI agents. The low-burning sconces outside of each cell did nothing to warm the hopeless dungeon. The fat guard unlocked the iron door to the empty six by eight room the giant had called home for many years and shoved them onto the cobblestone floor. They struggled to get to their knees as he studied the blond's curvy figure. Despite his Master's warnings lust engulfed him and he reached down and pulled her upright by the hair. When he cupped her breasts a woman in the adjacent cell stuck her head between the bars.

Get your hands off her, Munn shouted but failed to stop the giant.

If my Master didnt want you alive for CK's amusement I'd snap your fucking neck, Hong said and punched the agent in the mouth to send him back to the floor.

Let go of me, Lauren yelled and tried to elbow him in the nose but had to settle for stomping on his foot.

You stupid whore, Hong said and punched the back of her head.

Hong, you dirty, dirty boy, the woman in the adjacent cell said. You know what Ohanzee and Sister Angelica would say about this, dont you?

Mind your own business Anne, Hong said and tried to backhand her but instead hit the bars. If you say a word I'll throw you off the bell tower, do you hear me?

You wont be killing anyone if Angelica locks you up again now will you? Anne said and smiled. She was fifty something, rough around the edges but was still attractive because of her natural beauty and long gray hair. There were bags under her eyes and a scab on her lip.

Come on Hong, get outta there, the guard said as the other prisoners banged on the bars and chanted Anne's name.

Quiet down, all of you, Hong yelled. He stormed back down the hallway as the guard relocked the door. Several moments of uneasiness passed before the agent made eye contact with their intrusive neighbor.

Thanks, I owe you one, Munn said.

My pleasure, what are your names? Anne asked. Her cellmates studied Lauren who balled up on the cot with her head between her legs. The agent sat in front of her to block their view, pulled off his dark blue FBI jacket and draped it over her.

I'm Agent Munn and this is Lauren, he said and winced in pain from his chest wounds. His button down shirt had tears running across it with purple and green bruises surrounding the coagulating lacerations.

That looks painful, where's your friend James? Anne asked while keeping a beat with her hands on the iron running perpendicular to the bars.

How do you know about him? Munn asked while ripping the sleeves off his shirt.

I know all there is to know around this church.

Yeah, well whattya know about breaking outta here? Lauren asked from behind the agent.

I know its nearly impossible unless you have a secret, Anne said.

I bet you got a lot of secrets, huh? Munn asked. He tied the sleeves together at the cuffs and snaked the improvised bandage around his back. He brought it around his chest, made sure it was covering his open wounds and tied it while crying out in pain.

You bet I do.

And whattya want in return?

A shot at CK.

Why?

He killed my family at a campground in West Virginia so I joined Angelica's church to start over, Anne said and smiled. Little did I know that motherfucker was a charter member.

I'm truly sorry about your family... he's a sick, sick man.

Thank you.

If it's any consolation, I owe him a few rounds too, Munn said and tried to get comfortable on the single bed. So if the opportunity presents itself I'll make sure we both get our revenge, sound good?

Sounds great.

Now what's that secret of yours?

I know how to stop the lunatics running this church.

How?

Do you know who Phoebe is?

Yeah, the Greek deity, Lauren whispered.

Yes and no. She's actually a false idol who steals women's souls in exchange for more power in Hell but that's beside the point.

Then what's the point? Munn asked.

Sister Angelica is channeling Phoebe to stop Didanawisgi from reaching San Francisco because she just cant let go of her beloved congregation. The only thing keeping her from leading an insurrection against Master Bauta is his promise to reflesh her twins.

Okay but who's Didanawisgi?

An old Medicine Man who saved the Master's son from death not too long after the Civil War. In exchange, the Master promised to transport Didanawisgi's army out of Hell.

For what purpose?

To storm the Vatican and steal the third volume so he can give his warriors eternal life. His dream is to eradicate the white man and rebuild his tribe in the west.

It all sounds hunky dory but how do we use this intel?

Strike a deal with Didanawisgi.

How? Lauren asked.

Talk to James, he's the one learning how to use the Fire, not me, Anne said while pushing the dying burn victim off her cot. Besides, you already owe me a favor Agent Munn.

32

Omnipotens lucifer... si vocare te ad nos... sic potest magister... haec portal... Sanctificávit... Móyses... Amen, Didanawisgi said into the amorphous mirror on the opposite wall of his lair. The mosaic of broken glass reflected the decorated skeleton holding his tomahawk on his throne built from the jawless skulls of his enemies. In his other hand was a tarnished chain leading to a collar wrapped around Katie's neck. She stood by his side with her arm draped across his shoulders. A row of openings behind them let the crimson light of Hell into his chambers. Tarnished artifacts stolen from graves around the world were stacked in random piles. A stone banquet table covered with tablets written in dead languages was situated on the balcony facing the courtyard.

He tilted his skull when the mirror lost its reflective qualities and transitioned from a blinding light to Master Bauta lying in bed. The decrepit old man raised his arm to protect his eyes, slid out from under the covers and stood naked waiting for the underworld to come into focus.

Why are you summoning me at this hour? Bauta said with no shame for his wrinkled body.

Visions... Phoebe... she's coming, he said and began spinning his tomahawk. She's getting closer.

Yes, I know... I was just having a nightmare about her.

She's gaining strength, Didanawisgi said and pulled Katie over to the mirror. She draped both arms over his shoulders and ran her fingers across his ribs.

Hello Master Bauta, she said and cackled.

I have nothing to say to you woman, Bauta said and grabbed his staff to light his room with a new flame.

Does the spell work? Didanawisgi asked.

I dont know yet, we are running experiments on some prisoners now, Bauta said and rubbed the sleep from his eyes.

When?

I will know by the Sabbath, Bauta said with strength. I need all of Sister Angelica's congregation ready in order to transport your army here. Otherwise, you'll get trapped somewhere inside the Earth for eternity.

No... no time left, Didanawisgi yelled, cocked back and threw his tomahawk across his lair. It twirled six times before embedding into the igneous wall behind his throne. Splinters crawled up to the bone-covered ceiling. The splinters became cracks and the cracks became fissures as Katie scampered away in fear.

You'll be long gone before Phoebe reaches the black mountains, Bauta intoned and crept over to his bed.

You lie... ground shakes here, Didanawisgi said and sat in his throne. Katie reclaiming her position at his side.

Good night old friend, Bauta said, whispered a spell in Latin and the closing portal cut off the Medicine Man.

33

Wake up Munny Bunny, it's time for your flying lessons, CK laughed from the platform at the top of the south tower of the Golden Gate Bridge. Two of the Master's servants kept guard by the open hatch. He had the agent hogtied at his wrists and ankles and facing the sky with his right boot on his chest to keep him from going over the brink. Five hundred feet below vehicles of all different shapes and colors traveled northbound and southbound with no idea of what was unfolding above their heads. Forty mile an hour winds howled around the three feet wide steel cables and drowned out the San Francisco and Oakland nightlife.

I said wake the fuck up, he yelled with two hands on the nearest cable. He pumped his foot up and down to wake him from the nitrous oxide. We didnt drag you all the way up here just to toss you into the Bay.

Where am I? Munn asked as he opened his eyes. CK... what are you doing?

Look around Munny Bunny, he said and used his free hand to gesture at the Bay.

Oh no, Munn said as the cannibal knelt beside him.

I brought you up here to make a deal, he said and put both hands around his neck. Tomorrow we're gonna use your CB to call that hillbilly sheriff.

No... I wont do it... I wont let you hurt anyone else, Munn said with spit flying out of his mouth. Fuck you... you sick fucking wacko.

Okay, have it your way.

He took his hands off his neck and drew a switchblade from his front right pocket. When he depressed the faux silver button out came a six inch blade. He grabbed the zipper on the agent's dark blue slacks and went north with the brass. After he separated the fabric with his fingers he reached past his Fruit of the Looms and cupped his scrotum.

No, please dont, Munn said as his eyes darted to his own manhood and back to the cannibal. I'll do whatever you want.

Good, I'm glad you could see things my way Munny Bunny, CK said and squeezed. Like I was sayin, we're gonna talk Dwyer into bringin James to the Devil's doorstep tomorrow, okay?

34

Hong pulled on the chain anchored to the wall of Paytah and Yoki's tomb and fed it through the shackles around Lauren's bruised and chafed wrists. The giant took a medieval padlock and clasped the two different types of iron together but when he double-checked to make sure the binds were secure she let out a painful cry. It aroused him so he gave her a mischievous smile. She couldnt squirm away from his stinking breath as his dirty hands made their way past her midriff and to her supple young breasts. When he tried for a kiss she swung her right leg up and smashed his testicles with her bony right knee. He doubled over in pain as she broke his nose with her other knee. Blood sprayed onto the stone floor as Sister Angelica entered the crypt with a wooden bucket hanging from her right hand.

You goddamn rapist, she yelled and dropped the pale of soapy warm water. We never should've let you out of your cell.

I'm sorry Angie, I cant help myself, he said and used the back of his right sleeve to wipe his face. She cupped his chin in her soft hand and raised his oversized head.

There's nothing to be sorry about, freaks like you never know right from wrong, she said and used his hood to dab the blood from his crooked nose.

Angie, please dont send me back to my cell.

That's for Master Bauta to decide, she said and pushed him away in anger. Get out of here Hong.

Are you sure? he asked. Anzee said not to leave you alone or I'll be in trouble.

You'll always be in trouble so long as we allow you to live Hong, she said and ignored the girl while studying her skeletal twins lying on the stone table. But one more thing.

Yeah?

Thank you for bringing my husband back alive.

You're welcome Angie, he said and escaped down the corridor.

Are you okay? she asked the blond and grabbed the bucket.

No, I'd rather be dead than be down here, Lauren whispered and adjusted her shackles so they didnt cut into her skin.

Unfortunately you dont have a choice in the matter because I have plans for you. She wrung out the rag and began to wash Paytah. His bones were getting cleaner and cleaner by the day but still hadnt reached the desired color.

Plans?

Yes, I'm going to teach you how to speak with your mind, she said while focusing on his ribs.

My mind?

Yes, like this, Angie said, stopped scrubbing and closed her eyes. After several moments Lauren caught the faint echo of four words in the furthest recesses of her consciousness. They became louder and louder until the priestess' voice was crystal clear.

Can you hear me?

Are you in my head? Lauren asked with a puzzled expression.

Yes, but you dont have to talk, just think it.

Okay... like this?

Yes, good girl... now I want to tell you a story about my husband.

My eyes feel heavy... what are you doing to me?

Master Bauta was a Southern Baptist who left Arkansas after the Civil War... he ended up in New Mexico, started his own church and met a squaw who was banished from her tribe because of her drinking... the Master helped get her sober and they fell in love... after a small wedding and building their own church she got pregnant.

I think I'm gonna pass out.

Shh, just listen... one day after mass they were attacked by Apaches and she was struck in the heart by an arrow... Bauta played dead until the warriors left but knew time was of the essence if he wanted to save their baby... as the sun beat down on the him, the shadow of his burning church was cast onto his wife's dead body while he cut their son out of her stomach... after he snipped the umbilical chord with his pocket knife he looked to the sky and heard God say Ohanzee... Ohanzee... Ohanzee... when he couldnt find the town doctor, the sheriff pointed them toward a Medicine Man living in the abandoned cliff dwellings miles south of town... that crazy old Indian assured Bauta his son was going to be okay after spoon feeding him a strange concoction to quiet his crying... the two talked for several hours about the white man... his greed, the expansion west and how they were slaughtering tribes wholesale... before they parted ways Master Bauta asked him what Ohanzee meant... the Medicine Man said the English translation was shadow... his tribe only spoke it when describing warriors who can harness evil to do good.

Why did you tell me that story?

Because I want you to know that Ohanzee led me out of the shadows and introduced me to Master Bauta who taught me about the Fire... about Phoebe... about collecting souls for power... and now that I have control of your mind, you'll do exactly as I say or end up in a cell like Hong.. do you understand me Lauren?

Yes... I understand Sister Angelica.

The priestess hung the rag on the rim of the bucket and placed her right hand on the blond's head. After she used her thumb to pull her eyelids up she checked her dilated pupils, stood back and slapped her several times with a light hand. She showed all the signs of being under the priestess' control so she went back to cleaning Paytah and Yoki's remains.

35

Sheriff Dwyer, it's CK, come in you fuckin redneck, over, the cannibal said over the walkie talkie hanging off the sheriff's left hip. He sat in a window booth opposite James at Mike's Original Diner in West Oakland.

That really him? James asked and slammed his coffee cup down on the table, rattling their silverware and plates dirtied by half-eaten hamburgers and fries drowning in ketchup. Their menus were stuck behind a Seeburg tabletop jukebox but their selections hadnt played over the speakers mounted into the drop ceiling.

You mind turning that down sir? the Latina waitress asked while smacking on her gum with a Bunn coffee decanter in hand. It's loud enough in here, dontcha think?

Yes ma'am, Dwyer said. He yanked the CB off his utility belt and twisted the volume knob clockwise and held it close to his mouth. Come in CK, this is the sheriff, over.

Y'all want some more coffee? the Latina asked and rested her free hand on her hip. Huh?

No ma'am, keep the change, Dwyer said and slid a twenty across

179

the red Formica.

Thanks but we cant seat you next time if y'all wander in here looking like that, the Latina said and stuck the bill in her apron.

Duly noted, Dwyer grumbled.

They vacated the hectic restaurant filled with yuppies, Berkeley students and city workers on their lunch break staring at the disheveled Midwesterners. They hustled past the busboys and waitresses carrying full and empty trays and the line of impatient customers in the foyer. After they skipped down the front stairs they sat on the hood of their Ford. As they waited for the cannibal's voice a stream of vehicles raced up and down Peralta Street and seagulls screeched from Oakland Outer Harbor.

Hey Sheriff, I got Munny Bunny and sweet, sweet Lauren with me, CK said and giggled. We've been havin lots of fun, over.

Ask him if she's okay, James said, pacing back and forth in the parking lot.

CK can you please confirm that Lauren is okay? Dwyer asked, reaching out to stop the farmboy from adding to his anxiety.

They're fine but I need you to listen, CK said. We're in San Francisco at the First Church of Radiance but Master Bauta wants to exchange Munn and Lauren for the farmboy.

Whattya mean? Dwyer asked.

I mean we'll let them go if the farmboy comes to mass at three o'clock this afternoon, CK answered.

Why James? Over.

Because he's turnin into a powerful little farmboy... but I'll let Munny Bunny go over the details, CK said over the bad signal.

Dwyer, it's Munn, the special agent said with a beaten voice.

Munn, are you okay? Dwyer asked.

Just listen... come to the church this afternoon... no backup, snipers or funny business, promise?

Yeah, I promise.

Good, because CK's been torturin the FBI Agents who were monitoring this place.

Copy that but what about you? Dwyer asked but the channel went dead for several moments. Dwyer to Munn, come in Munn, over.

Sheriff, it's me again, CK said. Just bring the farmboy to mass and I promise not to eat Lauren for dinner, over.

I'm sorry James but if you want her back you're gonna have to dive into the belly of the beast, Dwyer said and plunged his hand into his front pants pocket to scrounge for change. Think it over while I call our friends back in Stratford County.

James stood outside the booth while Dwyer fed all of his coins into the silver slot of the AT&T pay phone and closed his eyes to recall the number of his office hidden somewhere in the recesses of his mind. After three rings the dispatcher picked up and connected him to Deputy Carls.

It's the sheriff.. no, listen goddammit, Dwyer said. He spotted two women in cloaks with decagram pendants hanging from their necks standing by the unmarked van they had abandoned in the redwoods. One was a redhead the other a brunette. Their bare feet were filthy. Mud was caked under their long toenails.

They're freakin me out sheriff, James whispered without taking his eyes off the Sisters.

Same here, Dwyer whispered, switched the phone from his right to left ear and dropped his free hand onto his revolver. Carls, listen, drop whatever you're doing and round up the missin Laredo boys' fathers and head to San Francisco... just fuckin do it Carls, over and out.

What are we gonna do? James asked as the sheriff slammed the phone into the receiver. They both turned to the women staring at them with blank eyes.

We're gonna get to that church before I shoot those two weirdos dead in front of this fine establishment, Dwyer said and they jumped into the cruiser. So, what's your answer?

I'll do it under one condition, James said and turned around in his seat. The Sisters were in the cab of the van.

Yeah, and what's that? Dwyer asked. He threw the V8 in reverse, backed up and signaled onto Peralta. After taking Mandela Parkway north he merged onto Interstate 80 with the van in his rearview mirror. The traffic was bumper to bumper and the stormfront had engulfed the Golden Gate Bridge.

If they dont release Lauren, promise me you'll burn that fuckin church to the ground, James said and the sheriff laughed while raindrops smacked the windshield. The two Sisters followed as splinters of lightening struck the bridge's orange girders. Thunder rattled the loose .357 rounds in the console of the Ford.

36

A little before three o'clock on Friday James sauntered up the front stairs of the First Church of Radiance. Sheriff Dwyer sat in the Ford on Steiner Street waiting for the farmboy to keep their end of the bargain. The two cloaked Sisters from the diner parked behind him, rushed over to the driver's side door and separated their cloaks to reveal their breasts. The sheriff honked his horn to scare them away and drove past the farmboy while tapping his left ear twice. The giggling Sisters hustled back to their stolen van and followed him down the block. A couple of Black women walking down the sidewalk raised their cloaks to reveal their unshaven crotches. Filipino twins and a Mexican woman on the other side of the street showed off their petite asses. They laughed and licked their lips as the gusts coming from the lingering storm tumbled leaves onto the church grass.

Better come inside before you get wet farmboy, a man said, opening the right cathedral door.

CK? James asked as the cannibal lowered his hood and smiled to reveal his perfect teeth. There were stitches on his face and his energy was lethargic.

Hurry up, we've been waitin on you, CK said and disappeared

into the narthex.

The farmboy double-checked his surroundings. Nine more Sisters had gathered around the neighborhood to show off their tattooless bodies. They undid the plaited ropes tied arounds their waists to show off their natural figures and extended their arms to welcome the rain. He took a deep breath and walked in as the booming of a well-played organ filled his ears. When he reached the nave he took a step back and a few hundred more Sisters glared at him from the rows of crowded wooden pews. The cathedral door he forgot to close slammed shut and the half-drenched Sisters from outside rushed past him adjusting their cloaks and filled the few vacant seats. None lowered their hoods when the haunting modal scale came to an end.

Welcome my child, Bauta said over the dead silent congregation. He sat in the highest chair before the altar with Ohanzee and Sister Angelica to his right and left. Please, come join us.

Where's Lauren? James asked without moving an inch.

Dont be afraid, your girlfriend will be here any minute, Bauta said while beckoning him with his staff.

Bring her out or I'm leavin, James said and took calculated steps backwards while the Sisters in the last few rows exited their pews.

I'm afraid you're never going to leave this church again, Bauta said as they surrounded him. They got closer and closer so he searched every direction for an escape.

Bring him to me, Bauta said and dozens of hands grabbed James' jacket, arms, legs and even his crotch. Their sharp fingernails tore past his stolen clothes and into his flesh. One came away with a handful of his brown hair and she raised it toward the fresco ceiling. They lifted the kicking and screaming farmboy into the air and walked him down the nave, up the altar stairs and dropped him at the Master's feet. Before he could get upright they tore off his jacket, belt and shoes. His dirty jeans and socks came next as the Master, bald man and priestess laughed at the skinny teenager. They ripped off his flannel and revealed a body mic taped to his chest with the connecting wire running to the radio transmitter situated in the small of his back.

Stop, Bauta said, stood and pulled the top piece of tape off so he could hold the microphone close to his nauseating old mouth. Sheriff Dwyer, are you listening?

He's long gone by now, James said and a sickness flowed through his veins. It told him to double over and vomit but the Sisters kept his arms trapped behind his back.

Keep your mouth shut farmboy, Bauta barked and brought the microphone back to his cracked lips. Sheriff Dwyer, dont bother coming back. Not alone, not with your friends from Laredo and certainly not with the FBI because our dungeon is full of anyone who has tried to betray us.

He dropped the device onto the marble floor, raised his left hand and snapped his fingers. The microphone exploded, a flame ran up the wire to the farmboy's back and exploded the transmitter. He cried out in pain as the Master sat and cackled with the bald man and the priestess.

Where's Lauren you fuckin bastard? James cried out as the Sisters tore off his underwear and left him standing on the altar in the nude. They retreated back to the empty pews while he cupped his penis and scrotum with his shaking hands.

Hong, bring me the blond, Bauta ordered without taking his eyes off the farmboy. And hurry, it looks like someone's chilly.

The congregation erupted in laugher as the giant carried a nude Lauren in his arms from the sacristy and placed her at the farmboy's feet. He held her and gazed into her drugged eyes.

You came back to save me, Lauren whispered and he kissed her full lips.

Of course I did, James whispered and met the Master's stare. What did you do to her?

Oh, you'll have to ask Hong, I dont linger down in the dungeon, Bauta said. The giant struck the farmboy on the back of the head with the butt of his wavy dagger to render him unconscious.

37

Eight servants carried the remains of Paytah and Yoki in two silver-handled oak coffins down the cavern trail and up the rock formation stairs. Master Bauta, Ohanzee and Sister Angelica stood waiting on the landing. When the Master nodded the bald man knelt beside the north refleshing decagram and the priestess knelt beside the south decagram. They spun the brass combinations built into the stands to the same sequence of numbers to set the diagonals of the ten-pointed stars into motion. The tarnished silver made a God awful racket transforming into five-pointed stars as years of dust floated to the ground. Four of the servants opened the first coffin, carried Paytah's remains to the north pentagram and Ohanzee strapped his wrists and ankles to the four outward pointing apexes with leather straps. His skull covered the upward pointing one. The remaining servants repeated this process with Yoki on the south pentagram.

Once finished the servants carried the coffins back down the stairs where Hong and CK were walking up the trail with James and Lauren in chains. The naked teenagers were slow-going up the staircase because of the tranquilizers sprinkled onto their last meal but managed to join the small congregation without falling down the embankment. The giant unlocked their cuffs, cradled James in his arms and hoisted him onto the backside of Paytah's penta-

187

gram. Ohanzee strapped his neck, waist, wrists and ankles down and Angelica duplicated this process with Lauren on the backside of Yoki's pentagram. Neither prisoner fought to break free as their unblinking eyes gazed down at the hundred feet wide petroglyph on the cavern floor.

How long ago were they drugged? Bauta asked. His hood was drawn and the white flame at the top of his staff pulled his face in and out of shadow. He wore a ruby ensconced silver pentagram around his neck and his fingers were heavy from his diamond, opal and emerald rings.

Less than an hour ago Master, CK said and bowed.

Good, let us begin, Bauta said and gestured to Ohanzee.

The bald man pulled his dagger from the brown leather sheath hanging on his hip and cut the farmboy's left wrist. An anxious stream of blood flowed into the silver chalice Angelica held with both hands.

Will you do me the honor my love? Ohanzee asked. He wiped off the curvy blade with the silk handkerchief he kept in his cloak.

With pleasure, Angelica said and smiled from ear to ear. She dabbed her right hand into the chalice several times. With a steady confidence she painted the Hebrew symbols for Leviathan on the farmboy's forehead, shoulders and thighs and an upside down cross on his bare chest. After the priestess repeated the drawings on the blond she drank from the chalice as did the Master, bald man, giant and cannibal.

It's time to put the Fire back into my grandchildren, Bauta said and raised the end of his staff to Paytah's skull. The flame leapt into his vacant eye sockets, sputtered and almost went out but he whispered the spell over and over until his bones came to life. The skeleton raised his skull and let out an elated shriek when his parents came into focus.

My dear Paytah, I'm so sorry I wronged you, please forgive me, Angelica said to her son and wept as the Master worked the spell on Yoki. After several moments of convulsing she came to back life and faced her brother but was still finding her voice.

You really did save their souls Master... I'm sorry I ever doubted your word, Ohanzee said and bowed with his wife.

Off course I did my child but my promise to reunite your family is not yet complete, Bauta said, handed the giant his staff and took the second volume from the bald man. He opened it to the section marked with one of Morfran's feathers and found the refleshing spell. After clearing his throat he recited the words and the energy on the landing shifted from euphoric to nervous.

Omnipotens Luciferum vocavi te enim declinastis ad servum Paytah Yoki atque Andrea, et Lauren est, Bauta said while conducting with his free hand. Quorum oculi etiam odore nasum iterum ore sapor iterum iterumque digitis aures Tange, Amen.

The others chanted along as James and Lauren's skin split down their spines, across their shoulders and at the back of their arms and legs. Their eyes, organs, tendons and veins detached and slipped through the diagonal bars of the pentagrams and found new life inside the twins. Arteries, tendons and muscles followed as their skin finalized their refleshed bodies. Their twitching limbs glowed and flashed in the areas where the Fire needed to repair the stolen systems.

Our children are alive again Ohanzee, Angelica said and ran her fingers over Paytah's handsome face. His dark eyes, long nose and high cheekbones drew from his father's Native American blood-line. Yoki was similar but her mother's beauty came through with her piercing stare, full lips and round face. Despite the absence of hair they were still gorgeous teenagers. When the moment was right Hong and CK cut them from the pentagrams and they fell into the arms of their parents who wrapped them in silk cloaks.

And now it's time to say goodbye to our Midwestern friends, Bauta said and walked around the pentagrams to face James and Lauren. Their bones were still wet from their flesh being ripped away but the flames in their off-white skulls burned strong. They fought their binds and snapped their jaws.

Master Bauta rapped his staff on the floor six times and began the conveyance spell. A ring of fire emerged around the perimeter of each pentagram and the diagonal bars evaporated to reveal a blazing tunnel cutting through the Earth. When the last words rolled off his tongue the writhing teenagers fell into the flames. The portals shut and the smoke rolled into the stalactites hanging from the ceiling of the cavern.

38

A skeletal hand the size of a truck blasted through the floor of a cavern throwing hundreds of naked women in every direction. Boulders ricocheted off the stalactites and back onto the broken human pentagram. Another hand shot through and ripped the crevice further apart and two horns followed by a skull with flaming eyes made its way into the sacrificial cavern. The behemoth stepped up and onto the limestone floor as the surviving women ran for their lives the way rats do in flooding sewers. When they escaped through the iron doors a steady beeping caught the behemoth's attention as it rotated to locate the source. Its folded wings raked the ceiling and floor creating plumes of dust as it took six steps to find C-4 blocks stuffed between two stalagmites along the north wall. There was more hidden in a crevice to the west and more near a pool of water to the south but time ran out and a chain of explosions flooded the cavern in fire.

Deputy Carls to Sheriff Dwyer, it's the Laredoans, over, Carls said over the walkie talkie in the sheriff's hands to wake him from the wicked nightmare on Monday morning.

Whattya got Carls? Dwyer asked, sitting upright on the uncomfortable pew. He had Saint Nicholas Church all to himself except someone had lit the candles around the Virgin Mary statue while he was asleep. Rain pelted the stained glass windows.

Sheriff, me and Deputy Johnson rounded up all of the missing boys' fathers and we're almost to Nevada. We'll probably reach San Franciscan in half a day, over.

Scratch that, I need you to meet me in Sacramento.

Sacramento? Over.

Yeah, we got a weapons depot to ransack.

Are you out of your mind? Over.

No, Carls, I'm not... besides, who named y'all the Laredoans?

Pablo's mom, I think her name's Sophia, over, Carls said and the metal doors to the church swung open.

Sheriff Dwyer over and out, he said, shuffling down the pew. He ran down the nave to meet the priest clutching his bloodstained stomach with his hands.

Help, O'Sullivan said with red spilling from his mouth as he tripped and fell on the carpet.

Son of a bitch, what happened father? Dwyer said as the barefoot redhead outside the diner ran through the doorway with a wavy dagger in her hand. The brunette followed with another dagger and they screamed at the top of their lungs in search of their wounded prey.

Drop your weapons, Dwyer said and leveled the iron sights of his Ruger on the redhead. When she didnt stop her maniacal charge he shot once and her brains landed on the south narthex wall. The brunette leapt over her sister's collapsing body and straddled the sheriff. She brought the dagger over her head but he fired into her stomach before she could pierce his heart.

Somebody... help me, O'Sullivan gasped as the sheriff rolled the brunette onto the floor. He took the priest's head in his hands and gazed into his fading eyes.

If... if they take your soul... you wont go... to Heaven, O'Sullivan whispered and drifted into the cosmos.

39

James and Lauren woke from their passage through the Earth lying face down in a field of bones. They were several miles from the make-shift city built into the east side of the black mountains stretching across the First Circle of Hell. Their souls kept their scorched frames animated as they staggered to find balance on the red sand riddled with massive skulls, ribs and vertebrates. Somehow their vacant eye sockets caught three skeletons riding fleshless horses approaching from the west. Neither could speak so they stumbled around the fossils and toward the refracted horizon where a large red star and a small orange star were rising into the carbon monoxide filled sky ending at the igneous ceiling. When they reached a river of lava they attempted to wade across but the current was too strong. They snuck along the bank for a quarter of a mile until discovered by the search party.

Halt, the decorated warrior yelled as the other two dismounted their horses, unraveled a mess of chains and shackled the teen-agers. They dragged them back to their horses, lifted them over their hindquarters and mounted the beasts without saddles. Bri-dles made of smaller chains went through their mouths, past their necks and back to the riders.

Good... now we ride, the warrior said and used the back of his spear to spank his beast. Ride, ride, ride.

Flames shot out of their horses' nostrils, down their cervical vertebrae and into their bare rib cages to power their journey through a dust storm created by poisonous winds rolling across the desert plains. Lightening bolts shooting from the black clouds highlighted by a dozen shades of orange splintered to the roofs of the approaching city. Acid rain came down in sheets as the warriors reached the teeming courtyard and halted before the feet of the enormous tribe's Medicine Man.

Welcome home, Didanawisgi said while twirling his tomahawk and holding the chain leading to Katie's neck. The decorated warrior approached him while the others jerked the prisoners from their gasping horses and threw them to the ground with no regard for their vulnerable condition. The Medicine Man let enough chain out so Katie could approach the farmboy. She knelt and cupped his chain to raise his skull.

Remember me? she asked with her tortured past buried deep in her crackling voice.

Katie? James asked without his old mouth, tongue and throat to pronounce the word.

Hello again farmboy, Katie said and pulled Lauren to her feet.

We found them... in the fields, the warrior said and set the bottom of his spear on the bricks.

Calibration's off, Didanawisgi said. Must fix... before my journey.

Before our journey, Katie added while studying the girl's frame.

Of course, Didanawisgi said.

Who are you? James asked.

Didanawisgi... your new Master.

Where... are we? Lauren asked with an infant's control over her distorted words.

Hell, Katie said cackling.

For how long? James cried out. He seized Lauren's hand in fear of the creature who destroyed his hometown abusing his girlfriend.

Forever, Didanawisgi said and the lingering crowd erupted.

After a slow rumble followed by a seismic tremor the Medicine Man led the teenagers into the makeshift city, through a network of shadowy tunnels lit by sconces hanging from the walls and into an overcrowded dungeon where fire pits illuminated the wall of cells. Long stretches of iron were welded together at imperfect angles to house hundreds of fleshless prisoners of every size, condition and time period of human civilization. They stood and clutched the uneven bars to study the teenagers.

Your new home, Didanawisgi said. The guard unlocked their cuffs and pushed them inside. Katie studied their cellmate with a tattered crucifix hanging from a silver chain around his neck.

Hello again, the skeleton said with a voice familiar to James.

Good morning John, Katie said and nodded as the guard relocked the one ton door. The petrified teenagers were left alone to fend for themselves as their cellmates surrounded them.

What's your name? the skeleton asked the farmboy.

James... and Lauren, he said as she cowered behind him. Yours?

Father O'Mally, the skeleton replied and pointed to the other prisoners. And that's Dan... Pablo... Dwayne... Teddy... Quentin... TJ... and Mac.

Dad? James asked and Dan embraced him.

Where's your mother? he asked with traces of his old voice left in the words.

Buried... in the redwoods, James said but their reunion was cut short by Dwayne, Teddy and Quentin attacking the farmboy.

You damned us... to Hell, Dwayne screamed.

Dan and Father O'Mally tried pulling his crazed old buddies off him. Lauren was thrown to the ground as their thrashing bones clanked against each other.

Help us, Dan cried out but Pablo, Mac and TJ couldnt stop the primordial fight.

As the creatures exchanged blows James knocked them onto their backs with a surge of fire. There was silence in the dungeon. The prisoners in the adjoining cell pushed each other out of the way and crowded the adjoining bars to witness his newfound power.

What was that? Quentin asked from his side as smoke rolled off his bones.

The Fire, James said and whispered a spell in Latin to grow a flame over his carpals. I'll use it... to resurrect you... and redeem myself.

40

Help, Angelica screamed and the word bounced around her bedroom, out the open door and up the stairwell where Hong stood outside the Master's chambers. Inside the candlelit room Ohanzee was studying the second volume but he dropped it, ran past the giant and down the stairs. He found Paytah and Yoki ripping hair from his wife's head and tearing her black silk cloak the way hungry wolves rip apart their prey. With patches of her gorgeous mane gone the twins brought her to the floor and shredded her skimpy bra and panties. She fought within an inch of her life to defend herself from their fingernails digging into her neck, back, arms and legs.

Angelica, Ohanzee cried out. He rushed into the room but couldnt get past his rabid children to save his wife. Hong, get down here.

The giant loped into the chambers and wrapped his enormous hands around their necks as they kicked and screamed. Their arms werent long enough to claw his boiling and leaking face. He inspected Paytah and then Yoki but the twins were not the same as before their deaths. The hair on their heads and eyebrows had grown back in sparse patches, their eyes were full of broken blood vessels and their stinking mouths were spewing obscenities forbidden by their parents.

What happened my love? Ohanzee asked but she ignored him whiles collecting her stolen hair off the floor.

Is she okay Anzee? Hong asked as the twins tried biting his forearms. The bald man fetched a throw from the chair by the window, draped it over the priestess and gave the struggling giant a puzzled expression.

I dont know Hong, Ohanzee said. He sat next to her on their disheveled bed as she studied the two piles of hair in her shaking hands. What happened Angelica?

They're possessed, she whispered with tears ruining her makeup.

Possessed?

Yes, possessed, she said and ignored their twins. I've seen that look in the eyes of the prisoners our Master experiments on.

What? How could you say that Angelica?

I was trying to show them pictures from their first birthday in Golden Gate Park when they attacked me, she said with a whimper. They're fucking possessed Ohanzee.

What is going on in here? Bauta said and shuffled her over to the giant. Those arent our children.

I'm sorry I left so abruptly Master but they were attacking Angelica, Ohanzee said while rubbing her back.

What? Why on earth would they do that? Bauta asked and motioned for Hong to lower the twins.

I saw them Master, Hong said. I saw them rip Angie's beautiful hair out.

Thank you Hong but no one asked for your opinion, Bauta replied and placed his hands on Paytah and Yoki's shoulders. He crouched and whispered something under his breath. A sudden transformation occurred and they scampered over to their parents.

Get your hands off me, Angelica cried out and raced to the mirror sitting on her vanity to cover her patchy hair with the throw. Those arent my children, those are demons.

Angelica, stop this at once, Ohanzee yelled while trying to comfort the scared twins.

Demons? Bauta asked with a sarcastic tone. I've seen demons my dear and my grandchildren certainly arent demons.

Hong, take them to the dungeon, Angelica said and stood in the doorway pointing down the stairs. Now.

The dungeon? Bauta asked and got in her face. How could you do that to Paytah and Yoki?

Because you promised to bring my children back and failed, Angelica yelled while slamming her fist on the door. Tell us Master Bauta, why did you put tortured souls into my children?

4

Looks like a couple of grunts, Dwyer whispered from his belly. He handed his Bausch and Lomb 10x50 binoculars to Deputy Carls and waited for him to wrap the plastic strap around his hand before lifting the optics to his tired eyes. The lanky German had a brown moustache, a weathered face and muscular hands from a childhood working in the fields around Stratford County. There was a cheap gold band around his ring finger and he stunk of Newports. He glassed the compound while rotating the focusing ring until two camouflaged infantryman with M-16's slung over their shoulders came into view. They were larger than life in the circular frames but had no clue the lawmen were spying on them from the top of the surrounding hill covered in sage brush.

Yeah but we're gonna need more firepower to take them out, Carls whispered and returned the binoculars.

No need, I got a better plan, Dwyer whispered and motioned to retreat. They belly crawled out of sight and duckwalked to a cluster of native oaks in need of rain. They knelt and the sheriff grabbed a stick and drew the fence, driveway and weapons depot in the wet sand with the help of the high yellow moon.

Whattya thinkin Sheriff? Carls whispered but an alarm went off a mile to the east.

Fuckin hell, Dwyer grunted and stood. He focused his binoculars on the Laredoans' pickup trucks parked half-in the north ditch of Fruitridge Road.

Probably Deputy Johnson's truck alarm again, Carls whispered and nudged the sheriff for the binoculars. I told that dumbass to disengage it from his battery before we got here.

Shit, Dwyer whispered and rubbed his temples. Get on the horn and tell him to draw attention away from this area.

After confirming the trucks were headed eastbound they revisited the hill but hit the dirt as one of the infantrymen started one of the olive drab Jeeps. Its headlights almost gave away their position. When they drove through the open gate the lawmen drew their service revolvers, jogged along the chain link perimeter and found a section where the ground was separated from the fence. They lifted it high enough for one another to crawl under and found the entryway unlocked. Once they darted past the front desk, conference rooms and a line of offices down a narrow corridor they found a set of locked steel doors marked ARMORY.

Find something to pry this sucker open with while I radio the Laredoans, Dwyer whispered.

You got it sheriff, Carls whispered, scurrying back down the hall.

Dwyer to Johnson, come in Johnson, over, he whispered into his CB while keeping his revolver pointed toward the ceiling.

Johnson to Dwyer, over, he replied through the distorted channel.

What's the status on those guards, Dwyer whispered and lowered the volume.

They trailed us for a few miles but turned around and are heading back your way, over.

Shit, y'all better get your asses back here then, over and out, Dwyer whispered as his deputy returned with a metal prybar.

I found it in the machine shop, Carls whispered, sticking it in the door jamb.

Wait, wait, wait, Dwyer interjected. He searched the walls for security cameras but instead found a horn mounted above their heads. When this door opens that siren's gonna go off, so let's split up and find some explosives and get the fuck outta here, kapeesh?

Kapeesh, Carls whispered. He took great cuation rocking the iron back and forth but still triggered the migraine inducing alarm.

Run, Dwyer called out. He led the deputy inside and went down the first aisle where rows and rows of metal shelves were stacked with BDU's, boots, night vision goggles, backpacks, body armor and helmets. There were countless boxes marked as ammunition, magazines, M16's, grenades, mortars and surface-to-air missiles.

You hear that? Carls yelled over the alarm and across the massive warehouse as gunfire was exchanged outside.

Yeah, keep lookin goddammit, Dwyer yelled back.

After searching a few more aisles he came across a palette of crates labeled C-4. They threw a box of blasting caps and a detonator on top of the wooden crate and carried it by the rope handles back through the building.

The shooting stopped, Carls whispered, trying to catch his breath in the foyer.

Something must be wrong, Dwyer whispered and approached the door with great caution. Oh fuck, come on deputy.

They left the crate inside and found shell casings and the grunts lying dead beside the bullet-ridden Jeep. Their eyes were still open and blood soaked their fatigues around the buckshot holes. The sheriff was praying for the fallen infrantrymen when two crew cab F250's painted maroon with tan Laredo Lumberyard stickers on the driver and passenger side doors drove through the open gate. Deputy Johnson, along with Esteban, Glen, Orville, Larry, Tom and Kenny, exited the Fords with their scoped rifles, shotguns and pistols pointed toward the sky. The shellshocked fathers wore trucker hats, deerskin gloves, camouflaged hunting jackets, over-alls, flannels, blue jeans and beat up leather work boots.

What the fuck happened? Dwyer asked the ashamed deputy as the fathers checked on the dying grunts for any signs of life.

Orville's rifle went off when we were gettin out of the truck... so these two fired on us, Johnson said while reloading his Remington 870 Express.

I'm so sorry sheriff, I thought the safety was on, Orville said and slung his scoped rifle over his right shoulder. He removed his hat to scratch his curly blond hair.

I told you twenty fuckin times to keep your finger off the trigger, Kenny said as the skinny farmer zipped up his dirty Carhartt.

Fuck, fuck, fuck, Dwyer yelled and marched over to Orville. Listen you stupid hick, if you pull that shit again I'll shoot you myself.

What's done is done... but these two will have died for nothing if we dont get those explosives to San Francisco and save our boys, Esteban pleaded to the lawmen.

I hate to interrupt but I hear sirens, Glen exclaimed.

So do I, Kenny said.

Larry, Tom, help Carls, Johnson get that C-4 into the trucks before we spend the rest of our lives in the prison, Dwyer yelled. They did as they were told and scrambled to escape the FBI racing across Sacramento County.

42

An army of female warriors riding fleshless stallions approached the black mountains with their skulls, hands and feet painted white and the rest of their bones dyed purple. All of the horses were done up in the same fashion except their bridles were done up in red. They kicked their calcanea into the beasts' exposed ribs and raised their hatchets, swords and spears into the blistering air. They cut through the field of bones and left behind a rolling cloud of dust from the shoeless horses kicking up a million years worth of broken fossils. When they came within a few hundreds yards of the makeshift city the citizens rushed to their open windows and balconies but didn't comprehend the army's primordial war cry. Stories below their Medicine Man walked into the courtyard holding his tomahawk and extended his left arm to halt the approaching warriors but they ignored his warning.

Luciferum vocavi vos omnípotens divideret terram cum abundantia mea liquefacta in ventrem trahat, Didanawisgi said under his breath and the wind changed directions affecting his headdress and jewelry. When the third repetition left his jagged teeth a crevasse grew between his feet, darted toward the warriors and splintered causing great chunks of the Earth to fall into the lower rings of Hell. They spun their bucking horses around and tried to bolt around the fiery lava spewing from the maze of cracks. When the last warrior drowned in the hardening magma the Medicine Man raised his weapon and celebrated with his howling tribe.

After returning to his chambers he was met by Katie and two of his servants guarding James and Lauren, the farmboy's best friends, Dan and Father O'Mally. He walked by the shackled entourage, sat on his throne of skulls and laid the tomahawk across his lap.

Bow to Didanawisgi... I said bow, Katie said and snapped their chains but they were still having trouble controlling their bones.

Why wont you bow? Didanawisgi asked. Answer me.

Time to negotiate, James said in defiance with Lauren standing behind him.

Negotiate? Didanawisgi asked and brought his tomahawk down on the right arm of his throne.

Bow first... or be desouled, Katie said.

Ohanzee... Sister Angelica... are betrayin you, James said while he knelt and dropped his skull with the others.

How dare you... this is heresy.

It's true, Lauren said.

Please listen Didanawisgi... please, Katie begged while loosening her grip.

Listen to them? Didanawisgi asked and rose. Phoebe's coming... no time for games.

I know, see? Katie said and flames enveloped her eye sockets. Silhouettes appeared of Sister Angelica channeling Phoebe in the catacombs below the First Church of Radiance. The priestess' words were distorted in the Medicine Man's mind but he still caught onto her betrayal. He stormed across the room and grabbed Katie's arm in anger.

This cant be, Didanawisgi said, studying the waning prophecy.

It can, Katie said. Trails of smoke rose from her skull after she arrested the flames.

We have a plan... to stop Phoebe, Lauren said.

A plan? Didanawisgi asked.

Yes... will share... on one condition, James said.

Anything.

Reflesh us.

Deal.

43

Drink from the Chalice of Radiance my beloved Sisters, Angelica said as she dipped the medieval silver cup into the stoup filled with wine and handed it to the skinny Black girl at the beginning of the crowded line running down the center of the nave. Drink and the spirit of Phoebe will flood your minds, bodies and spirits and you will see the future. A future without the curse of masculinity, a future where our ever-growing congregation will live in the New Garden of Eden. Drink my beloved Sisters, drink the blood of Phoebe on this Sabbath and the future I speak of will be yours.

Claudia made the organ in the balcony come to life as the Sisters tilted the cup back, rejoiced in the psychedelic wine sliding down their throats and accepted the silk rag Ohanzee handed them to dab their lips. After they handed it back to him they motioned the Sign of Radiance over their forehead, shoulders and chests and re-folded their hands. They joined the queue to the sacristy where Hong stood guarding the hidden door to the winding stairwell.

This way Sisters, Bauta said, beckoned them with his staff and gave the go ahead to the giant. He spun the decagram handle clockwise and counterclockwise until it transformed into a penta-gram. Once he opened the heavy door he walked into the dark, lit the first wall sconce and descended the limestone stairs. The bustling line of Sisters passed by the giant without question as the spiked wine caused their skin to tingle, a kaleidoscope of colors to flood their eyes and toxins to spoil their veins. Those with the least amount of faith in the Fire panicked but the most brainwashed sang about Phoebe. When Angelica and Ohanzee passed by Hong he shut the hidden door behind him but before he could lock it a revolt took place outside of the catacombs.

No, Diya cried out while collapsing in the entryway. Two Sisters with brown and red hair tried to console her but the wine was having the same effect on them. This isnt right... something's not right... I'm not feeling radiance... I keep seeing a giant creature with wings... hundreds of skeletons... and San Francisco in flames.

Stand up and continue or be punished, Angelica said to her.

You... you put something in that wine didnt you? Diya asked in a drunken stupor. Tell us what it was Sister Angelica... tell us or I'm not going any further.

Keep moving Sisters, please keep moving, Ohanzee said but couldnt get past them as their wild and tripping eyes told them he was a demon. The brunette and redhead scratched his face and pushed him against the wall in a psychotic frenzy. He used every ounce of restraint he could muster not to retaliate for fear of a full scale revolt.

We have to keep moving Hong... so dispose of them before you join us in the cavern... just dont let anyone see, Angelica whispered to him as she grabbed her husband's shaking hands.

Anything for you Angie, he whispered but the brunette and the redhead became violent with him.

My beautiful Sisters... dont go any further, Diya cried out and her incoherent diatribe echoed down the congested stairwell. They're leading us to our deaths... stop... they've betrayed us all.

You three better calm down or I'm gonna feed you to CK, Hong whispered to them when the congregaion was out of view.

Hong... what are you doing? Diya asked as he grabbed the brunette and redhead by their long hair. Stop... I have to warn the other Sisters... they're not going the right way... the radiance is toward the light not the darkness... please Hong... let me go.

Everything is going to be okay Diya... trust me, Hong whispered. Without hesitating he smashed their faces together until they fell unconscious on the stairs.

44

There were a couple of miserable FBI agents in parkas guarding the chained and padlocked First Church of Radiance when two crew cab F250's driving north came to a stop on Steiner Street. The downpour was relentless so the locals were already inside their cars, restaurants and homes when the left passenger side windows of the trucks lowered and two scoped hunting rifles rested on each sill. Without warning the out of synch gunshots sent the water-logged crows perched along the roofline, on the railing and in the sidewalk trees back to the sky. The agents rolled down the stairs and onto the pavement with blood leaking from their chests and into the surrounding puddles. After pulling the box of explosives, two crowbars and a set of bolt cutters from the bed of the first truck the sheriff, his two deputies and the well-armed Laredoans raced across the intersection with the supplies. Lightening struck the silver decagram sitting atop the highest peak of the cathedral when they reached the stairs followed by a wave of low thunder.

God only knows what's on the other side of these doors so let's treat this place like the Alamo, Dwyer whispered to the others as Deputy Carls handed him the bolt cutters. Distant sirens drifted into the empty neighborhood as the sheriff put his weight into the cutters. It took three attempts to break the heavy lock. He tossed the tool into the bushes, collected the loose chain and grabbed the right handle while drawing his Ruger. When gave the go-ahead Deputy Johnson swung the heavy and creaking door open and everyone rushed the sacred space. He slammed it shut, snaked the chain through the interior handles and used his Stratford County issued handcuffs to lock them inside.

Anyone home? Dwyer asked the abandoned cathedral. When they received no reply they took to clearing every nook and cranny.

Sheriff, I think we've been duped but I did find this, Carls said and handed him a wine-stained chalice.

Use those crow bars to pry some of the pews from the floor... and barricade the entryway, Dwyer said to the fathers without turning to them as he studied the relic. Looks like our missing friends drank the Kool-Aid before they locked the place up, huh?

Apparently so, Carls replied. Sirens, slamming doors and scurrying men penetrated the stained glass windows boarded up from the outside.

Sounds like the cavalry's here, Johnson said and the deputies helped the fathers carry the splintered pews to the narthex.

In here, a woman cried out from the sacristy. Help... I'm in here.

Carls, Johnson, come with me, Dwyer whispered, dropped the chalice and pointed his revolver past the altar. He tiptoed into the sacristy, grabbed the pentagram handle of the hidden door and confirmed his deputies had his back before yanking it open.

Stay down, Dwyer ordered with his revolver pointed at the Indian woman lying on the stairs. Her light brown face was swollen and bruised. The crotch of her torn cloak was covered in blood.

Johnson, help me carry her, Carls said while holstering his Glock.

What's your name ma'am? Where is everyone? Dwyer asked as the deputies laid her on the floor.

Diya... my name's Diya, she gasped with a thick Indian accent. They're in the cavern... all of them.

Talk to me Diya, Dwyer said, resting her head on his knees. Slow down and tell me what happened. Come on now, talk to me Diya.

Be careful down there... she's coming, Diya said, studying the cracks in the ceiling.

Who's comin? Dwyer asked and checked her neck to find a weakening pulse.

Phoebe... Phoebe's coming, Diya whispered as the lawmen stared into her dying eyes.

45

Follow me, Katie said as the guard held the door open and marched James and the other prisoners out of their cell, through a crowded tunnel lined with skeletal warriors and into the forge where the Medicine Man was overseeing a team of blacksmiths wearing medieval aprons. They were busy fitting them with helmets and body armor straight from the ringing anvils where they hammered the mild steel into shape. When the warriors were battle-ready they grabbed one of the razor sharp swords, spears or axes and stuck their other arm through one of the shields waiting on the cooling racks. After they passed by the bellows, vats glowing with molten metal, blast furnaces and casts they exited the bowels of the black mountains chanting a medieval war song.

Arm yourselves, Didanawisgi told the Laredoans as Katie strapped on a breastplate.

Why? James asked.

Disguise from Bauta, Didanawisgi said and almost lost his balance.

What was that? Lauren yelped as the blacksmith stopped fastening her armor. The ground shook, fragments of lava rock fell from the ceiling and plumes of dust flooded the overcrowded forge. Fractures climbed the walls and a seismic tremor knocked the Black Mountain Army off their feet.

Phoebe's close, run, Didanawisgi yelled, grabbed Katie by the left humerus and pushed the other warriors out of the way. He ripped the torch from the wall sconce and instructed the waiting queue to vacate the infernal room. Panic became hysteria as women and children flooded the exits of the quaking city. The Laredoans followed the Medicine Man as his torch waned until crying, rampant footsteps and squealing horses greeted them in the courtyard. The mirror atop the black crystals had shattered and he picked up one of the shards to find his own reflection. Memories of his time in the southwest told his conscience to save his people before they were slaughtered by the imminent behemoth.

Bring the horses, Didanawisgi yelled at his army.

Why? one asked but received no reply.

When the entire tribe was assembled in the courtyard and the fleshless stallions circled the crowd he raised his right index finger to his jaw. The silence was deafening while he contemplated his words and cut the air twirling his tomahawk.

Women and children... take the horses... to Fourth Circle, he said to his people and they erupted in protest.

Silence, Didanawisgi screamed. Obey me... or join Phoebe. After a few altercations they obeyed and the warriors helped their kin onto the team. When the time came the fathers and sons grasped the bridles, said their goodbyes and smacked the hindquarters of the horses. They rode toward the setting suns and away from the Black Mountain Army who would transport them back to their lands in the southwest once they eradicated the white man.

46

By the time Master Bauta led the Sisters past the great cavern doors they were bug-eyed, drooling and swaying down the trail in a catatonic stupor from the side effects of the sacrificial wine. After they came to a stop before the embankment the Master ascended the stairs and stood behind the pulpit. The flame at the end of his wooden staff illuminated the flowstones, stalactites, stalagmites, helictites, soda straws and columns surrounding the carved pentagram. The earth tones shot into the Sisters' retinas where their lenses converted them into a spectrum of electrical impulses. Ohanzee and Angelica led the congregation onto the petroglyph edged by servants.

Please undress my Sisters, Bauta said as Ohanzee, Sister Angelica and Hong stood behind him on the landing. Undress and let go of your beautiful bodies so your souls can walk in the New Garden of Eden where Phoebe is waiting to grant you eternal life.

As you wish Master Bauta, the Sisters said in harmony, undid the plaited ropes around their waists and dropped their cloaks. Their skin goose pimpled because of the cool air so they rubbed their arms to stay warm. None of their genitals were shaven or even trimmed, matching their unkempt armpits, eyebrows and leg hair. Their bare feet were mud-stained from the wet trail.

Please, show them their positions, Bauta said to his servants hiding in the shadows along the north and south walls and they walked across the petroglyph.

They escorted the first group of twelve Sisters onto one of the diagonal channels of the petroglyph and coerced them onto their backs head to toe with their arms folded across their bare chests. Another dozen went over the next thirty-six degree angle and another and another and another until completing the five-pointed human star. After making a few adjustments to the overlapping bodies they escorted five groups of twelve Sisters to connect the apexes of the star by curving their bodies. When the final group was in place the women spread across the entire sixty-six foot wide human pentagram were peaking on the wine.

Thank you for so many years of dedication to the First Church of Radiance my old friends but the time has come for us to part ways, Bauta said to his servants as they retreated into the shadows. I wish you a safe journey to the New Garden of Eden, goodbye.

As they had practiced dozen of times before the servants wielded the wavy daggers hidden under their cloaks and waited for their Master's signal. When he smiled they rested the blades under their chins, cut their own throats and blood soaked their chests and trickling down their legs. One by one they dropped the knives and grabbed their necks in a futile attempt to stop the mass suicide.

I cant watch anymore, Angelica confessed and buried her face in her husband's chest.

I know it's painful but it's vital if we want to reach Italy, Ohanzee whispered and embraced her. Life will be better there, I promise.

Now I want to tell you a little story about the history of this church my beloved Sisters, Bauta said to the comatose women.

Back in the sixties, there was a hippie couple who joined our little congregation on California Street out of desperation. John and Katie were addicts so we fed and clothed them and provided them a warm place so they could get clean. After a time of sobriety and dedication to my teachings, he relapsed when she became pregnant. So on a cold and rainy October night back in 1969, I offered my congregation the same wine you drank in the cathedral this morning and led them to our basement. We tied Katie to a pentagram and John stood by drugged out of his mind as we sacrificed her to Phoebe... but Phoebe never made good on her promise of eternal life. In fact, our house burned down, Hell swallowed Katie and John stole my book of spells. Soon after, Ohanzee and Sister Angelica transported me to another place and time before the authorities could throw us all in prison for murder. So please allow me to apologize for Phoebe my dear, dear Sisters because her promise of a New Garden of Eden was a lie... but I swear to each and every one of you... she will welcome you in Hell.

By the time his last words reached the congregation's ears they were paralyzed from the neck down but still able to move their eyes and mouths. As they filled the cavern with primordial screams hundreds of crows flew out of the north tunnel and perched on the stalagmites surrounding the petroglyph. One separated from its flock and circled the landing.

Magnus et potens Lucifero, Bauta said and Morfran landed on his left shoulder while he kept a four-four time signature by striking his staff on the rocks. Observantiam commutat placet, Sanctimonialis of Radiance Didanawisgi enim est in terris apud inferos exercitus, Amen.

Ohanzee and Angelica stood on either side of him repeating the spell, clapping their hands and stamping their feet in unison as Hong cowered in fear behind the sacrificial pentagrams. After six repetitions a series of seismic tremors caused fissures to race under the reeling congregation, up the walls and across the ceiling. They closed their eyes and braced for death as the petroglyph changed from limestone to magma to flames in seconds as one-hundred and twenty betrayed Sisters were transported through the Earth.

47

Carls, Johnson, you and half of that C-4 are comin along with me, Dwyer ordered as Orville and Kenny used their crowbars to open the wooden crate. The rest of you stay up here but do not, I repeat, do not shoot unless the Alamo is compromised. I'll bet my last dollar that our friends are down these stairs, any takers?

How can I collect if you dont make it back up here alive? Glen asked and handed him the remote detonator.

Well I guess you'll have to make your way down there and find my wallet, Dwyer retorted and stuffed the little black box into the front left pocket of his shirt.

Who do you think you're fooling Sheriff? Esteban asked as the other fathers gathered around with betrayed expressions on their faces. You're fucking using us as cover while you save Dan's son James but what about my boy Pablo?

Yeah, what about Quentin? Larry asked in anger. Mac? TJ? Dwayne and Teddy?

Trust me gentlemen, James will know where they are, Dwyer said and walked into the sacristy to throw a mauve cloak over Diya.

Carls, Johnson, you guys comin or not?

The sheriff led them down the winding stairwell with his Ruger aimed past the fading torches spaced along the curved wall. He clicked on his Maglite and shined it at the ceiling where cobwebs stretched from corner to corner. The clickety-clack of toenails on the limestone pulled his attention back to the stairs and he caught dozens of rats scurrying past their feet in the beam. A dozen more steps and they found two Sisters propped against the north wall outside the catacombs. Their necks were swiveled past their natural positions but their eyes were still open.

Cover me, Johnson whispered and nudged the brunette with his work boot. He did the same with the redhead to no effect.

Check their pulses, Dwyer whispered.

They're goners sheriff, Carls replied and stood to avoid more of the rats.

All right, leave them, Dwyer whispered. He stepped over their cold legs and used the curved wall as cover.

After leading the deputies past dead torches he reached a closed dungeon door. He approached it with great caution and reached for the pentagram handle. Without warning it swung open and hit him square on the nose, knocking him on his ass. From the entryway CK squeezed three rounds out of Agent Munn's 9mm Glock before the sheriff returned fire. One of his hollow-points hit the cannibal in the right knee.

Dont fucking move, Carls said and rushed in to find him writhing on the floor. He kept his shaking M16 aimed at his forehead.

Cuff him to the cell, Dwyer said and swung his Ruger's cylinder open to empty the casings. Johnson, guard the door while Carls and I check for friendlies.

You got it sheriff, the deputy said, used the entryway for cover and pointed his M16 and Maglite down the dark stairwell.

Hello again CK, Dwyer said and picked up the little brown bottle with the crude label marked CYANIDE lying on the floor. Were you using this to marinate your victims?

Yeah but Munny Bunny still tasted like shit, CK said with bits of flesh stuck in his teeth. He tried to laugh but screamed when Carls undid the belt wrapped around his waist.

Whattya doin? CK asked while clutching his leg.

Dont worry, we arent gonna cut your balls off, Carls said and wrapped the belt around his thigh for a tourniquet.

Even though we have every right to, Dwyer said but when he set the poison down two sets of hands bolted out of the closest cell and grabbed his arm. Paytah and Yoki jerked him against the rusty bars and scratched his face. They spit and snarled but could only yell obscenities because of their limited mental capabilities.

Let him go, Carls said and fired a warning shot over their heads.

The twins released the sheriff and scampered under their cot but kept their eyes on the lawmen. When he focused his attention to the other cells he was horrified at the aftermath of CK's addiction. There were doors still locked and some left open and prisoners lying on the floor with foam bubbling from their mouths. Death hung in the air as rats hurried in from the stairwell to join the dozens already feasting on the butchered corpses.

Down here, a man whispered from the last cell on the right.

I know that voice, Dwyer said and found a fortysomething man curled up in the fetal position on the floor. He was using an FBI jacket as a blanket.

Munn? What did CK do to you? Dwyer asked. He pulled the unlocked door open and rushed over to comfort him. A cloud of flies was buzzing around the agent's back.

Just listen, Munn whispered without opening his eyes. Take the... twins hostage... use them to get... James and Lauren.

Where are they? Dwyer asked as Carls lifted his jacket to reveal rectangular pieces of flesh cut from his shoulder. The unbearable stench made the deputy cover his nose.

One more... thing, Munn said and gestured toward the adjoining cell. Let Anne out.

What's he talkin about? Dwyer asked the gray haired woman surrounded by dead and dying cellmates.

He owes me a favor, Anne said as Munn went into cardiac arrest.

Come on Munn, dont you fuckin give up goddammit, Dwyer begged and slapped his face but didnt bother to pull the walkie talkie from his hip. We can get you out of here, wake the fuck up.

He's gone sheriff, we gotta keep goin, come on sheriff, Carls said and faced the woman. Anne, where are the keys?

In his cloak, Anne said and pointed at the fat guard sitting lifeless in his chair down the hall. Sorry, I couldnt reach him.

The deputy retrieved the cast iron ring and tried every key until the last told the door to open. He drew his Glock on the other prisoners and promised to shoot if they attempted to escape or harm her. They obeyed so he relocked the door once she was safe down the hall.

Come on Anne, we'll get CK on our way back up, Dwyer said from the entryway as his deputies waited in the stairwell.

I'll meet you on your way back up sheriff, Anne said, picked up the bottle of cyanide and smiled at the terrified cannibal.

48

Phoebe's here, Didanawisgi yelled as the Black Mountain Army raced onto the courtyard and arranged themselves onto the curves and diagonals of a giant petroglyph. Their helmets, armor and shields strapped to their frames wouldnt protect them from the behemoth clawing her way through the preceding Circles of Hell. The volatile ground sent the warriors to their knees but the Medicine Man stood tall as toxic gases shot from the fissures speeding toward the makeshift city at his back.

Where you going? Katie shouted at her new lover from one of the apexes of the five-pointed star where she was saving him a space.

Quiet, he commanded and the flames in his eyes were almost put out by the gale force winds from the upside down tornado swirling over the opening pit. It pulled sand, fossils and igneous rock into its funnel until a hand made of skeletons stuck its clawed talons into the adjacent field of bones. The behemoth heaved herself from the tunnel, shook the lava off her bones and extended her featherless wings.

Didanawisgi, Phoebe screamed across the plains. Her control over the Fire powered hundreds of the human-sized skeletons locking their hands and arms to comprise her axial and appendicular divisions. They howled the Medicine Man's real name in unison and snapped their jaws as he rushed to Katie's side.

Nos, nomine Niger exercitus vocat Archangelum Lucifer et transfer ad primum ecclesia foret, Amen, he chanted and raised his tomahawk. The warriors caught on and did the same with their weapons and shields.

Phoebe beat her wings, climbed the sky and covered several miles in seconds. Flames filled the circular and diagonal channels of the petroglyph but the army was unaffected by the pentagram-shaped inferno. When the behemoth generated enough speed she dove at a forty-five degree angle, extended her arms and opened her clawed hands while collapsing her wings down her back.

After the army repeated the invocation six times beams of light shot from the blazing symbol, into the air at obtuse angles and blinded Phoebe. She covered her eyes and expanded her wings again to slow her chaotic descent but was incapable of changing directions fast enough before crashing to the ground. Several dozen skeletons couldnt hold on and were left in her wake as she tumbled toward the army.

The First Circle of Hell unleashed enough lava to transport the army into the cavern below the First Church of Radiance and return with the one-hundred and twenty sacrificed Sisters.

Welcome home, Phoebe said to the smoking congregation as they flailed around the circle of cooling igneous rock trying to locate her with their vacant skulls. Now join me... for revenge.

One by one the Sisters came to their senses, sauntered over to her and expanded her mass by locking hands with the pre-existing skeletons on her legs, torso and arms. When all were attached she twisted her horned head to the ceiling miles above, flapped her wings and rocketed into the sealed but destabilized tunnel. Using her talons and hooves she burrowed her way toward San Francisco in a fury of vengeance.

49

It's good to finally see you again, Bauta said, strolling down the rock formation leading to the burning petroglyph. Didanawisgi was holding a chain connected to Katie's neck restraint in one hand and his tomahawk in the other. At their backs were one-hundred and eighteen warriors whose helmets, body armor, shields and weapons were shifting from glowing red to iron black. Whiffs of smoke rolled off their bones, up to the ceiling and around the stalactites. The army studied the cavern as their lungless ribs took in the clean air and their fleshless bones absorbed the low temperature. When the Master reached the edge of the petroglyph Katie lunged at him with her razor sharp talons but the Medicine Man retracted her chain and she landed on her back.

Are you still mad about what happened back on California Street in the sixties my dear? Bauta asked her in a condescending tone.

You sacrificed me... sent me to Hell, Katie yelled as the Medicine Man dragged her kicking and screaming back to his side. I want you... Ohanzee... and Angelica dead.... I want revenge.

Didanawisgi, it appears your pet needs discipline, Bauta said and they laughed at the thrashing creature.

Ignore her... we must talk, Didanawisgi answered with embers falling off his armor.

Of course, how could we possibly let anyone spoil our reunion? Bauta asked as he clutched his staff with one hand and lowered his black hood with the other. What troubles you old friend?

Traitors, Didanawisgi said and pointed at Ohanzee and Sister Angelica standing at the edge of the landing.

What did you say? Bauta asked and raised his free hand in defense.

How dare you, Angelica screamed but the bald man kept her from running down the rock formation in a fit of rage. Hong came out from behind the refleshing pentagrams with a strange expression on his face.

That's a very serious accusation, Bauta said. He slammed his staff down on the limestone to generate a roaring flame.

You heard me, Didanawisgi said and opened his left palm. See?

Master Bauta, send him back to Hell before he destroys everything, Ohanzee said and Hong put his hands on the couple's shoulders. They tried to escape but couldnt break his impossible grip.

Silence, Bauta said and a fireball shot from the top of his staff but dissipated before the stalactites. Didanawisgi has a right to clarify his accusation.

He has no autonomy here, Angelica said but Hong covered her mouth. Ohanzee became violent, kicking and elbowing the giant.

I said silence, Bauta said waving his index finger at the priestess. Didanawisgi, if your evidence is faulty I will desoul you... do you understand me?

Of course... Master Bauta, Didanawisgi said and sparks flew from his fingerstips.

Go on then, state your case.

With pleasure, Didanawisgi said and a fiery silhouette of Sister Angelica channeling Phoebe in the catacombs danced in his palm. Her words were distorted in the Master's mind but her betrayal was without question. He faced the terrified couple as the priestess' tears rippled down Hong's fingers.

Didanawisgi, may I ask who brought this evidence to you? Bauta asked without taking his eyes off her.

My new friends, Didanawisgi responded. The rows of warriors behind him parted so two teenage skeletons could make their way to the front.

And who might you be? Bauta asked.

James and Lauren, James said. He took off his helmet and flames emerged in his eye sockets to mimic the Medicine Man's prophecy. Katie's did the same and, one by one, the entire army's.

Hong, seize the traitors, Bauta called out and scaled the rock formation. When he reached the landing he brought Ohanzee and Angelica to their knees with his mind. They clutched their stomachs and screamed out for help but the giant peered down at them with a smile.

He's lying Master... Didanawisgi's playing tricks on your mind, Angelica said between gasps. I... gave you everything... my life... my twins... my congregation... why would I betray you?

I can name a million reasons why, Bauta said. He stepped onto the landing and used his staff to bludgeon the bald man in the ribs. But you Ohanzee, why have you betrayed me?

I'll do anything... anything you ask... just please... please dont hurt my wife and kids, Ohanzee said and grabbed his cloak. He was refused with the butt of his staff.

This is all your fault Master, Angelica screamed as she writhed on the ground. You tortured us for decades... you lied about Paytah and Yoki... you should be the one to die... Hong, let us go... it's Master Bauta you want... not us.

Hong, after you've shackled them ready my sword, Bauta said gazing down at the paralyzed couple. And make sure it's sharp enough to cut through both of their necks.

50

Sweet Mary, mother of God, Dwyer whispered to himself while holding Paytah and Yoki captive behind an outcropping of rocks at the west end of the cavern. They were bound at their wrists, gagged and blindfolded and it took what little strength he had left to keep them from getting free. He gazed past the trail cutting through the maze of stalagmites and to the landing where Hong was running a sharpening stone down a medieval sword. With each stroke sparks reflected in Ohanzee and Angelica's eyes as they stood on their knees with their hands tied behind their backs. Master Bauta stood behind the pulpit leading the Black Mountain Army below in a Latin prayer of death from the second volume. The malicious words echoed back to the sheriff and made him want to retreat but when Deputies Carls and Johnson returned from planting the stolen C-4 along the north and south walls he found hope.

The charges are all set, Carls whispered as they crouched beside him. I dont think anyone saw us.

If they did then we'd already be dead, Dwyer whispered struggling to keep the twins from giving away their position. Wait here.

He grabbed the chain running through their handcuffs and used them as a human shield to walk down the trail. When the Master's voice reached the twins they made a God awful racket trying to escape the sheriff.

Ahh, what are you doing down here Sheriff Dwyer? Bauta yelled and approached the west edge of the landing.

Negotiating, he said and brought his revolver to Yoki's temple as she screamed through her gag.

Come closer, Bauta demanded and reignited his staff to get a better view of the hostages. He squinted and shook his head.

What's so funny?

You came all the way down here to make a deal with two demonic children? Bauta asked. Sheriff Dwyer, I am disappointed.

I'll blow their fuckin heads off if you dont hand my people over, he said and cocked his Ruger.

You would be doing us all a favor, Bauta said as Didanawisgi and Katie led the Black Mountain Army into the maze of stalagmites. Little by little the warriors crept forward until the sheriff stepped back with the twins in tow. Ten skeletons surrounded him. Two were adults and the rest teenagers in size.

Sheriff... it's James, he whispered and the sheriff lowered his Ruger in shock. The Master seized the opportunity, raised his staff and the twins burst into flames.

No, Angelica screamed from her knees. Her twins tried to escape the inescapable pain but their linked restraints caused them to topple onto the trail. The blaze chewed through their blindfolds, gags and cloaks as they screamed at the top of their smoke-filled lungs.

You heartless bastard, I'll kill you, Ohanzee yelled at his father while the flames turned Paytah and Yoki into carcasses.

No my child, you've always been the bastard, Bauta said and stood over the bald man and the priestess. The bastard I pulled from your mother's stomach to save you from certain death so many years ago... the bastard who couldnt retrieve my book from Laredo without endangering our church... the bastard who sneaks around behind my back plotting my assassination with your bitch of a wife... Ohanzee, all I've ever wanted is to find the third volume and share eternal life with you and your family... but you have spoilt my plans for too long... Hong, do me a favor and cut this treacherous bastard's head off.

As you wish, Hong said, raised the sword over his head and paused at the enormity of his situation. Time stood still. Didanawisgi and Katie cackled as the couple dropped their heads in defeat.

Now, Hong, now, Ohanzee screamed and the giant swung the blade with all of his might and beheaded the Master.

Two streams of blood shot from his severed neck as his head bounced down the rock formation stairs and came to a stop before the sheriff and the ten skeletons on the trail. They gazed into the Master's eyes in horror. His eyelids twitched, mouth remained open and blood trickled from his nostrils and ears. His coarse white hair was cut to the same length as his vertebrate, carotid arteries, muscles and skin.

Kill him, Didanawisgi screamed and pointed his tomahawk at the awestruck giant standing atop the landing with the bloodstained sword in his hand. The warriors scurried around the stalagmites to claw up the rock formation as Hong cut the bald man and priestess' binds. This gave the sheriff enough time to pull the detonator from his pocket and run back down the trail with James, Lauren,

TJ, Mac, Teddy, Dwayne, Quentin, Pablo, Father O'Mally and Dan in tow.

Blow it sheriff, blow it, Carls screamed and the deputies opened fire on the pursuing warriors. The shots did nothing to stop them except splinter their bones and pierce their armor. The sheriff led the resurrected skeletons past his deputies and through the cavern doors where he waited everyone was in the stairwell. He screamed for them to climb the stairs as he slammed the doors shut and took cover in the corner. After flipping the first switch on the detonator he shielded his head with both arms. The charges placed along the cavern walls exploded, sent cracks up and across the ceiling and dropped stalactites onto the warriors. Hong shielded Ohanzee and Sister Angelica from the firewall with his massive frame.

5

Anzee, you alive? Angie? Hong asked, pushing the rubble off his own burned and battered body. The cavern was pitch black except for a scattering of flames along the walls. He hacked the cavern dust out of his lungs and tripped over the Master's staff sandwiched between two boulders. Using all of his strength he pulled it free, tore a piece of fabric from the sleeve of his tattered cloak and wrapped it around the fat end. He drew the Zippo from his cloak and lit the improvised torch. Strange noises told him to breach the edge of the landing and explore the maze of stalagmites where he once played hide and seek with Paytah and Yoki. Instead he found dirt, rocks and boulders shifting as the buried warriors tried to unearth themselves. Half a dozen fleshless hands were the first to break free followed by their fiery skulls lighting their escape. Faint cries for help brought him back to his hunt for the bald man and the priestess and he wedged the staff between two rocks and lowered his ear.

Hong, help me, Ohanzee cried out from underneath the rubble.

I'm coming Anzee, Hong yelled and tore at the stones. They flew underneath his legs the way dogs kick dirt from a hole.

Hurry, Angelica's under me, Ohanzee pleaded as the torchlight caught a glimpse of his desperate face.

Dont worry, I wont let you die Anzee, Hong yelled as he cleared a opening large enough to put his arms through and grabbed ahold of the bald man's cloak. With his legs on opposite rocks he pulled him from the wreckage and tossed him aside to reveal the smothered priestess. Her face was bloody and covered in grime. The giant shoved his fingers into her mouth to remove the blockage but she was still unresponsive. He heaved more rocks away, reached down and almost broke his back setting her next to the bald man. While keeping ahold of her with his left hand he reared back with his right and smacked her in the middle of her back. After three tries out came a throatful of pebbles and dirt and saliva followed by her first breath in several minutes.

Get away from me Hong, Angelica said and spat up bloody phlegm as her husband dusted off her patchy hair and cloak. I'm alive... I'm alive.

Thank you for saving her, Ohanzee whispered and a smile revealed his soiled teeth.

Anything for you two, Hong said but manic digging down the embankment interrupted their reunion. He picked up the torch and found dozens of the frantic skeletons almost out of the debris. Boulders were rocking back and forth and dirt was being tossed aside as they howled for freedom. Closer to the covered trail Didanawisgi was using his tomahawk to shovel himself out the ground. A few yards away Katie was using both of her arms to push away the rocks on her sunken ribs. She raised her skull and shrieked at the giant but something cutting through the Earth stopped all of the creatures in their tracks.

Phoebe? Angelica asked between painful tears as the surrounding rocks vibrated and dust floated into the air.

Yes my love, Ohanzee said.

There's a secret tunnel, Angelica said as the bald man pulled her arm around his neck.

Where? Hong said and brought the torch closer to light their faces.

Under the pulpit, Angelica said. The giant handed the staff to the bald man, put his back against the sculpted onyx and inched it north with his legs. Hurry, she's getting closer.

I'm trying, it's so heavy, Hong gasped, reclaimed the staff and stuck it between the base and the closest boulder. He put his weight on the cantilever and the pulpit toppled down the rock formation.

Look, she was right Anzee, Hong said and ran his fingers along the edges of a trap door encased in the limestone.

Quick, open it, Ohanzee urged with hope of escaping the doom rumbling below their feet. The giant found the circular handle built into the opposite end of the hinges and raised the corroded iron door. He grabbed the torch to light the opening wide enough for his broad shoulders.

Hong, watch our backs, Ohanzee said and crouched to help his wife onto the carved stairs. She placed her dirty hands on either side of the hatch, found her footing and disappeared in the dark. The bald man stepped down but stopped to take the staff. When the giant was eye level with the landing he reached up, grabbed the iron handle on the underside of the hatch and surveyed the cavern. The ferocious tremors caused the compromised walls and the ceiling to drop into a crevice opening in the center of the maze of ruined stalactites and stalagmites.

52

The sheriff paused outside the dungeon as the voice of a crazed man begging for mercy came through the locked door. He tried the decagram handle but had to settle for the barred window near the top to witness the horror of Anne cutting CK's left ear off with the dead guard's dagger. The buck naked cannibal was shrieking with skin missing from his face, chest, arms and hands and foam bubbling from his mouth. She stuck the dagger in her rope belt, drew the bottle of cyanide from her cloak and dosed his open wounds to exact her revenge. A torch sconce fixed to the cell he was handcuffed to lit the strips of flesh lying in the pool of red spreading across the floor as he convulsed from the poison.

Anne, get the fuck outta there, Dwyer yelled and slammed the butt of his revolver against the door.

Just leave her sheriff, we already set the charges, Carls shouted with Johnson by his side and the resurrected skeletons further up the pulsating stairwell. The deputies shined their flashlights past the dungeon but the heavy smoke made it impossible to identify who or what made it out of the blown cavern. They pointed their M16's into the darkness but there was only the clickety clack of strange footsteps to target with their metal sights.

I'm not leaving Anne, Dwyer said without acknowledging the C-4 packed into the corners of the entryway.

Sheriff Dwyer? she asked. Her face, hands and feet were stained red. Her mauve cloak had turned dark purple from the barbaric surgeries she had performed on the cannibal.

Help me sheriff, CK yelled with primordial fear in his eyes. I cant take any more pain... you gotta stop this crazy bitch... please.

Crazy bitch? Anne asked and brought the blade to his Adam's apple. With one stroke the small amount of blood left in his body spilled down his stomach and groin as he spat out the rest begging for mercy.

They're right behind you sheriff, Carls yelled. Two different pairs of flaming eyes cut through the smoke but the deputies couldnt get a clear shot because of the shaking stairs.

Unlock the door Anne, Dwyer yelled and she ran to him while wiping the blade on her thigh.

Before she could unlock the door a tomahawk whirled through the air, lodged into the sheriff's stomach and sent him to his back. When the two skeletons reached the dungeon Katie strangled Anne's guts with her mind. Without letting go of the bloody knife she dropped to the dungeon floor clutching her midsection. Didanawisgi put his left foot on the sheriff's shoulder and drew his weapon free to send blood streaking across the closest wall.

Fire, Carls yelled at Johnson and they emptied their clips on the approaching creatures. Their bones splintered and broke from the wave of .223 rounds but didnt stop their ascent.

With the broken chain still dangling from Katie's neck restraint she wished for the plague to fill their bellies. They dropped the M16's and rolled down the stairs in agony but the resurrected skeletons behind them were unaffected by her black magic.

Katie, James yelled at the creature responsible for destroying his life. The farmboy raised his arms and a fire shot from his bony hands. It struck her and the Medicine Man and they toppled down the stairwell. He and Lauren ran to the sheriff's side to try and keep his intestines from spilling out of his gaping wound.

Take this, Dwyer whispered and handed him the detonator.

Not leavin you, James said and took it as the tremors became worse and a crack made its way down the ceiling.

Go... I'm already dead, Dwyer whispered as the color disappeared from his face.

Come on, Lauren said and tried getting him upright.

Save yourselves, Dwyer whispered and gazed into the farmboy's fire eyes. If you cant... then blow the whole fuckin place.

I will, James promised. They caught up with the resurrected skeletons in the lightless cathedral where the terrified Laredoans hid behind the remaining pews in the nave. They pointed their weapons and flashlights at the creatures in fear of being slaughtered.

James and Lauren, he said and gestured to the others who displayed silhouettes of their former selves in their fire eyes. And that's TJ... Mac and Teddy... Dwayne, Quentin and Pablo... Father O'Mally... and Dan.

Pablo... is that really you? Esteban asked and shined his Maglite on his son.

Yeah, it's me, he said with his mangled voice. The horrified fathers studied what was left of their kin until the cavern doors collapsing echoed up the stairwell spoiled their reunion. James and Lauren dragged the marble stoup from the altar to barricade the hidden door in the sacristy and retreated behind a pew.

What are you doing? Tom asked with TJ by his side.

Take cover, James warned and the others raced to join them. He raised the detonator, flipped the second switch and the explosion blew the lead door off its hinges sending flames, masonry and black smoke into the nave. Moments later the FBI Director of San Francisco demanded they surrender through a squelching mega-phone. The Laredoans peered through the cracks of the boarded stained glass windows.

Jesus, there must be hundreds of people out there, Larry said as helicopters circled the church. Dozens of agents with their pistols drawn used their unmarked Chevys for cover. The local police had Bush and Steiner Streets shut down but the locals still crowded behind the orange and white barricades.

They were trying to gas us before y'all arrived but stopped when we told them we rigged the cathedral with enough C-4 to blow the whole goddamn neighborhood, Tom said and pointed out the charges along the baseboards of the north and south aisles with his flashlight.

We still need a way out, Orville insisted and shouldered his rifle. Glen, what are you doing? Esteban asked.

They're watching us, he said as he snuck up the altar stairs and stopped before the glowing decagram mirror. Four cloaked figures wearing silver Venetian masks were standing in a gloomy Roman cathedral facing the Laredoans.

Who are you? Lauren asked and placed her bony hand on the cracked glass.

I'll be asking the questions young lady, Pulcinella said. Can one of you infidels please tell me where Master Bauta has gone?

53

Sister Angelica guided Ohanzee and Hong through the secret tunnel, up three flights of crumbling stairs carved into the Earth and to the trap door under the ambulatory on the west end of their church. Water trickled out of cracks in the ceiling, streamed down the walls and collected in puddles. Desperate rats scampered across their muddy feet. The air was cold and wreaked of San Francisco's garbage. The priestess grabbed the waning torch from the giant and scaled the staircase leading to a rusty old door with a decagram lock encased in the middle. A muffled explosion beyond the tunnel almost knocked her down but she managed to regain her footing. She worked the combination with the help of the torchlight.

Keep quiet, I can hear voices in the cathedral, she hissed and raised the squeaky hatch. The giant grabbed Master Bauta's staff, dropped it into deepest puddle to extinguish the flame and ignited his Zippo.

Careful my love, Ohanzee said to his wife and the giant followed them through the opening and into the cubbyhole. There was a silver mechanism encased in the plaster as tall and as wide as her face. When she worked the handle mounted on the side a series of gears spun the horizontal rod responsible for opening two peeping holes connected to Phoebe's eyes on the ambulatory mural. She hugged the wall as the flashlights in the Cathedral shone on her squinting face.

What do you see? Ohanzee asked from her right side and Hong on her left. The flicker of the lighter brightened the cubby hole.

The resurrected teenagers... their fathers... and the priest, she whispered and let him take a peek.

They've rigged explosives... and they're well-armed, Ohanzee said while crouching to line up his eyes with the peep holes.

Fuck, now what? Hong moaned but there wasn't enough room in the cramped space to change places so he let out a sigh.

Quiet you idiot, Angelica answered.

I'm sorry.

The both of you shut up, Ohanzee demanded but was patient closing the mechanism. We need a plan or we're gonna have to retreat into the cavern.

Phoebe will be here any minute, Angelica whispered as the time between the tremors decreased with each passing moment. Fuck, what are we gonna do?

Use these, Hong suggested and drew the two volumes from the pockets stitched into his oversized cloak.

I cant believe it, Ohanzee whispered and studied the tattered arti-facts. I cant believe you saved them Hong.

Wait my love, Angelica muttered and kissed him on the lips.

Promise me we'll start over when we reach Italy... have more babies... and live forever.

Of course, Ohanzee promised and stroked her sparse hair while staring into her deep eyes. He grabbed the handle and closed his eyes to pray before opening the secret door. They crept around the high altar but startled Orville as he was rigging C-4 to the back of the decagram mirror. It took him a moment to make sense of the cloaked strangers before grabbing his rifle lying on he marble floor. It was just enough of a delay to allow Hong to snatch the stout farmer by the neck with both hands. The giant waited for the bald man and the priestess to pass by before dragging him down the altar stairs.

We've got company, Kenny yelled and the Laredoans surrounded them. The skeletons blocked the narthex so they couldnt escape out the cathedral doors.

Hand over the detonator, Angelica said.

Why? Kenny asked as Hong lifted Orville up and into the air. The farmer kicked his feet and tore at his hands.

Or my friend will snap his neck, Ohanzee said.

Stand down, James said but the Laredoans were hesitant to lower their weapons. Go on... stand down.

We'd like to make an offer that could benefit everyone here, Angelica said and smiled.

And what could you possibly have that we need? Glen asked with sweat running down his back.

These, Ohanzee said and raised the volumes the way preachers raise their hands to energize their congregation on a balmy Sunday morning.

The books, Lauren said with excitement as an invisible wave of poison reached the Laredoans.

And what good are those? Kenny asked as his M16 weighed heavy and legs turned to jelly.

With the spells contained in these books we can keep the skeletons trapped under this cathedral from spilling onto the streets of San Francisco, across America and eventually the world, Ohanzee said and lowered them.

And if we don't accept your offer? Esteban asked and put both hands on his knees trying not to vomit.

Then the opposite will come true, Angelica said and laughed as Hong lowered Orville but kept both hands on his neck. The farmer gasped for air and his face changed from beet red to pink.

She's not lying, James said and walked in front of the Laredoans.

You sure about that? Glen asked with both of his shaking hands still on his shotgun.

Yes, James said and twisted his skull. See?

Dear God, Kenny said and caught the silhouettes of Phoebe standing over the demolished church. The farmboy faced the others so they could gaze into the prophecy.

So, do we have a deal? Ohanzee said, stacked the books on top of one another and brought them to his chest.

No deal, James said and raised the detonator.

You're willing to destroy these books and all the power contained in them... just to kill us? Angelica asked and retreated to her husband's side.

Yes, Lauren said and put her arm around the farmboy.

Reflesh us... or no deal, James said.

How? Ohanzee asked. It's impossible without bodies to sacrifice.

With this, Pulcinella said from the mirror. He raised the third volume to confirm its existence.

How did you retrieve it? Angelica said, ran to the portal and put her hand on the glass.

We have our ways.

Please forgive us for not knowing Master Pulcinella, Angelica said, dropped to her knees and clasped her hands. We thought it was still locked up in the Vatican.

Quiet, Pulcinella said, stuck the book in his cloak and readjusted the ornate silver rope around his waist. Master Bauta kept it a secret from Ohanzee all of these years because he never really trusted your actions.

We're sorry Master, we only wanted to give our children eternal life, Ohanzee said and joined his wife.

Quiet I said, Pulcinella yelled and his words echoed around the smoky cathedral. We will reflesh you but only because we need the other volumes to unlock the salvation spell.

Thank you Master, Ohanzee muttered and put his arm around his wife. Our souls and the souls of the children we have in the future belong to you.

That goes without saying, Pulcinella said. But there's just one thing I need to know before we join you in San Francisco.

Of course Master Pulcinella, what is it? Angelica asked.

Tell me, what happened to Master Bauta? Pulcinella asked close enough to fog the glass. He placed both of his hands on the frame.

We cut off his fucking head, Ohanzee declared and slipped the books into the pockets of his cloak. So from now on you can call me Master Zanni.

54

Master Pulcinella stepped through the decagram mirror, bowed to Master Zanni and Sister Angelica and studied the resurrected skeletons guarding the Laredoans painting a six foot wide pentagram in the center of the Nave. After giving the creatures a slow nod he returned to the portal and helped Masters Moretta and Brighella enter the cathedral. Gnaga was the last but she carried a Venetian mask. The tarnished silver had two mischievous eye holes and an elongated nose but stopped below the nostrils to leave its wearer with an exposed mouth.

This is for you Master Zanni, protect it with your life, Gnaga said with a Middle Eastern accent. She handed it to the bald man and lowered his hood with her porcelain-colored hands.

Thank you Master Gnaga, it's been a grueling journey, he said, adjusted the straps and raised his hood. His wife burst into tears and clutched his dirty right hand.

Congratulations my love, Angelica whispered while staring into his eyes and gave him a long hard kiss.

Welcome to the Circle of Fire, Pulcinella stated. He clapped with the others but their celebration was cut short by another violent tremor. Masters, please take your places.

What about us? James asked as the Laredoans stepped away from the finished sigil and directed their Maglites at the skeletons.

Lie down head to toe, Moretta instructed with a deep Russian accent and motioned to the pentagram. The rest of you fetch them something to wear.

It required two skeletons to cover each of the five diagonals by lying across one another to complete the human star. Once the Laredoans emerged from the sacristy with stolen cloaks the Masters stood at the five apexes, locked hands and closed their eyes. Hong put his heavy arm around Angelica and for once in their long and volatile relationship she embraced his protection.

Nos, Circulus Ignis insequi, accitis ex urbe hac sabbato principem tenebrarum, Pulcinella chanted in unison with the other Masters. Quaeso uti ignis ad reflesh James, Lauren, TJ, Mac, Teddy, Dwayne, Quentin, Pablo, O'Mally Patre, et ignis de Dan.

They repeated the spell five more times and on the sixth try the Laredoans' flashlights sputtered and quit, the cathedral rose in temperature and sickness found its way into their fragile bodies. They shook and smacked the Maglites on the palms of their hands but nothing brought them back to life. The tremors were back to back to back as ages old dust, plaster, furring strips and laths fell from the mural stretching across the ceiling and onto their heads.

What's goin on? Orville asked but nothing stopped the Masters.

Quiet, James insisted. He twisted his skull while raising his right index finger to his battered jaws as the Laredoans stood in awe of the ritual.

Sparks flew out of the resurrected skeletons' eyes. Flames grew in their empty cavities to consume their extremities. Their nervous, cardiovascular and muscular systems swallowed their bones and new skin extinguished the drowning flames. A strange orange light shot from the orifices where their eyes, ears and sex once belonged until they returned to their original form. Tiny hairs sprouted from the millions of follicles covering their bodies as they blinked and wiggled their fingers and toes.

Rise from the ashes of the Fire and enjoy the rest of your spared lives, Pulcinella said, broke hands with the other Masters and led them to the foot of the altar. The Laredoans rushed over to cloak their refleshed family and friends but had difficulties communicating with them because of their raw mouths, throats and lungs. Dan was helping Lauren to her feet when James checked the condition of the burnt detonator in his tender hand.

Dont worry, we were just leaving, Master Pulcinella said and smiled at the farmboy.

Goodbye, James whispered with a cracking voice after coughing several times and stuck it in his cloak.

For now, Pulcinella said.

The inevitable earthquake struck and splinters grew in the center of the charred pentagram and shot across the floor. The stained glass windows exploded, the statues of Phoebe broke apart and the Stations of the Decagram fell from the north and south aisle walls. As the foundation shook the chains running through the cathedral door handles broke apart and gave the Laredoans an escape route.

55

Into the portal, now, Pulcinella yelled at the other Masters as the pentagram tainted floor tumbled into the chasm. Phoebe's giant left hand composed of five skeletons for each phalange, five for each metacarpal, one for its wrist and dozens more for its radius and ulna reached through the fiery opening and seized Sister Angelica and Hong. The behemoth dragged them into the tunnel she had burrowed through the cavern, dungeon and catacombs to reach the cathedral.

No, Zanni screamed and dove to grab his wife's reaching hands but missed her by inches. He used his feet to keep from falling into the catacombs as the unbearable heat burned his hands and arms. The marble floor was breaking apart around him as the pews, bibles, statues, candles, stoup, organ, highbacked chairs and pulpit slid into the widening pit.

Leave her Master Zanni, she's gone, Pulcinella yelled across the room as he stood with his one foot already in the mirror and his left hand on the frame. Come, before it's too late.

Angelica, Zanni cried out as the behemoth stood with her hooves planted in the cavern and wings closed on her back. When she howled in triumph his silver mask protected his face from her searing breath but his cloak caught fire. Sister Angelica and Hong screamed for the last time when she opened her fanged mouth and bit their heads off. She tossed their limp bodies to the swarming warriors who had freed themselves from the wreckage of the C-4.

Ohanzee, Phoebe shrieked and extended her skeletal frame but missed the escaping bald man by inches. He extinguished the flames on the way to the mirror and found the other Masters waiting for him on the other side.

Take my hand, Master Pulcinella said and breached the plane as the portal shut faster than a guillotine. He pulled with all of his might and the bald man landed on the floor of a Roman cathedral. He scrambled back to the mirror with both hands on the edging to say goodbye to the First Church of Radiance but was heartbroken by his own reflection. Second-degree burns covered his head, soot had discolored his silver mask and smoke rolled off his black cloak. He began to weep as memories of migrating to California with his father in the late eighteen-hundreds, meeting Angelica in Haight Ashbury in the 1960s and playing with Paytah and Yoki in Golden Gate Park enveloped his mind.

There will be more than enough time to grieve Master Zanni but for now I need you to follow me upstairs, Pulcinella said while squeezing his shoulder.

Of course, Zanni said and they escorted him out of the nave of the anonymous cathedral, up three flights of stairs and into the open-air bell tower with a three-hundred and sixty degree view of a bustling Rome. To the west a crowd was gathering around Saint Peter's Square as Pope Saint John Paul II began the morning mass. Birds flew from one monument to the next as the rising sun cast the Eternal City in the Holy Spirit.

That's where we'll find the third volume, Pulcinella said and pointed to Saint Peter's Basilica.

Then... what were you holding... before you refleshed the Laredo-ans? Zanni asked. To his surprise Moretta and Brighella seized his flailing arms.

That? Pulcinella asked. That was just a decoy.

You betrayed us? Why? Zanni asked and his shock became rage. He fought to break free but Gnaga still managed to pull the first and second volumes from his cloak. After checking their contents she handed them to his new Master.

I'm truly sorry but it was the only way we could get them back to Rome safely, Pulcinella said and laughed with the others. You understand, dont you Master Zanni?

56

The surviving Laredoans escorted their delicate friends down the front stairs as aftershocks multiplied the fissures running across the sidewalks and adjoining streets. The FBI, police and crowd of hundreds scattered to avoid the lava spewing from the cracked Earth as the leafless trees snapped, telephone wires broke and windows shattered in the apocalyptic neighborhood. They hobbled past the San Franciscans left behind, killed by the stampede or trying to crawl from the chasms and went north on Steiner Street. The ensuing aftershocks sent them crashing to the pavement. When they tried to continue the eardrum shattering roar coming from under the cathedral made them cover their ears. The intersection of Pine and Steiner Streets was almost clear of people when Phoebe reached the nave.

Blow it James, blow it, Orville screamed as the Laredoans caught a glimpse of the behemoth's horned skull through the open doors. Enough flames were burning in her eyes, mouth and ears to shoot yellow and orange rays of light in every direction to blind any survivors for several blocks in every direction.

Everybody get down, James yelled and they took cover behind an overturned FBI van. He yanked the detonator from his cloak, flicked the third switch and the explosion overwhelmed the structure, disintegrated the roof and broken masonry, shingles, mortar, glass, wooden beams and ruined decagrams as far as a mile. The foundation collapsed but the behemoth expanded her wings across the pit and planted her hooves in the dungeon to stop herself from falling back into the cavern.

We need to get the fuck outta here, Kenny shouted as a group of crazed middle-aged women shuffled down Steiner Street.

Wait, who the hell's that? Dan asked because of his developing vision. He picked up a severed piece of rebar to defend himself as the others raised their firearms.

Dont shoot, that's our wives, Glen said and the fathers and sons met Sophia, Val, Amber, Mary Sue, Jan and Veronica below the flickering street light. They cried tears of joy and embraced one another as James, Dan and Father O'Mally spotted Phoebe clawing her way out of the demolition. The behemoth stood tall as smoking debris rolled off the hundreds of female skeletons making up her frame. When she couldnt find her prey she zeroed in on the Laredoans and lumbered north on Steiner Street.

Run for your lives, Dan yelled. He tried to guide his son to safety but the farmboy slithered out of his arms.

No, James said as the others recoiled in horror.

She'll destroy you, O'Mally cried out as the behemoth came to a stop before the farmboy.

No... no she wont, James said and held out his hands. With the last of his strength he created a flame large enough for the behemoth to comprehend his prophecy. He closed his eyes, turned his head and extended his arms so it wouldnt burn his hair, skin and cloak.

Where's Master Zanni? Phoebe asked him, spreading her wings to cast the Laredoans in darkness. Her skeletal frame tossed their skulls back and forth while snapping their jaws. They squirmed to attack the Laredoans but were bound by her spells.

Rome, James said and a silhouette of the Vatican being stormed by thousands of armored skeletons appeared in the flame.

After several failed attempts she reclaimed the sky, flew over the blinking Golden Gate Bridge and crossed the Atlantic Ocean. The reunited Laredoans retreated to their damaged trucks as the Black Mountain Army remained buried under what was once the First Church of Radiance.

Thank you for taking the time to read SKELETONS: Part Two: The Bald Man, please leave us an honest review on Amazon when you have time. Join our mailing list at skeletonshorror.com, follow us on Instagram at @skeletons_horror and watch our content on YouTube on the Skeletons Horror channel.

Andrew Reeves grew up in the rural town of El Paso, Illinois, where his family operated a farm for over one hundred years. After graduating high school in 1995, he majored in Visual Communications at Northern Illinois University and then worked as a graphic designer in Chicago. In 2003, he moved to the Echo Park area of Los Angeles, became disillusioned with advertising and released his first record as a musician, 1048 West Kensington Road. He relocated to Austin, Texas in 2007 to play live music and released Somewhere in The Middle of Nowhere and Where the Greed Won't Grow. In 2009, he returned to California and produced the guitar, bass and drums album New York City.

While taking a break from music in 2010, he created the "Black" series of paintings in his Glassell Park studio. The concept for SKELETONS was born during meditation and fleshed out with charcoal drawings that appeared in an international art show. Part Two: The Bald Man is the second novel in The Rapture Trilogy, preceded by Part One: Laredo and to be followed by Part Three: Revelations. He plans on later living in the Abiquiu area of New Mexico to write The Indian Wars, a post-Civil War western that will reveal the origins of the Master and the Bald Man.

www.ingramcontent.com/pod-product-compliance
Lightning Source LLC
Chambersburg PA
CBHW052033240626
47153CB00006B/2063